"How ironic," Darcy said slowly, trying to hang on to her temper. "You despised me for being willing to marry Evan to solve my problems. Now you're suggesting the same thing for yourself."

At first she thought she'd scored a direct hit.

"That was different," he explained, recovering smoothly. "I simply thought it was selfish of you to take advantage of Evan's infatuation." Miles hitched one long leg over the other and smiled, but it didn't blunt the sharp edge of his words. "With the bargain I've proposed, no one is taking advantage of anyone."

She flushed, knowing full well the subtext of his message.

Ever since she'd arrived, he'd treated her with contempt, up to and including the interlude in the pool last night. Perhaps— a sharp pang crossed her chest—that had been the most contemptuous moment of all.

Books by Kathleen O'Brien

KATHLEEN O'BRIEN

bargain with the wind

Harlequin Books

TORONTO • NEW YORK • LONDON
AMSTERDAM • PARIS • SYDNEY • HAMBURG
STOCKHOLM • ATHENS • TOKYO • MILAN

Harlequin Presents first edition April 1991
ISBN 0-373-11355-2

BARGAIN WITH THE WIND

CHAPTER ONE

"JUST GET OUT. Go now, before my finger slips and somebody gets hurt."

Infuriatingly, the man in front of her didn't move, unless his popping eyes and gaping jaw could be considered movement. Hoping she looked as menacing as the cops on television, Darcy dramatically extended her arm to its full length. "I said—get out!"

When he still didn't budge, she had to bite back a scream of exasperation. For pity's sake, how drunk was he? The gun was heavy, and her upper arm was beginning to ache. Even worse, the sweat from her palms was making it slip. She meant to be aiming it at his heart, but its snub nose kept ducking down toward his kneecaps.

Finally he frowned, awareness apparently seeping in, even through the whiskey vapors that clouded his brain.

"Is that a *gun?*" He squinted, his forehead furrowing as he tried to handle the unexpected twist. Clearly he wasn't accustomed to having his seductions thwarted at gunpoint.

She didn't answer. She just raised her brows and held her aching arm steady.

"Well, hey now, sugar, let's don't overreact," he said, automatically backing up, but keeping his eyes on the wavering metal snout.

"Hey, you want to be left alone? No problem. I'm a reasonable person." He gestured vaguely toward the gun, as though to point out that Darcy certainly wasn't. "You could just have asked me to leave."

"I'm asking you now." Darcy raised the gun and narrowed her brown eyes. "Leave."

"No problem," he repeated with feeling. The brick path must have seemed a mile long to him, but finally his heels found the curb. With a groan of relief he turned and bolted, racing toward the red convertible he had left waiting down the block.

Thank heaven! Darcy thought, watching him go. She let her arm drop and shook it to loosen the burning muscles. Now that he was safely away, she almost felt sorry for him. Poor fellow, he'd probably be sick in his little car. Fear and liquor didn't mix. Poor—was it Tom? No, maybe this one was Roy. Or Bob...

But what did it matter what his name was? The men her stepfather hung out with at the country club all looked alike to her. Maybe they sat down at the club's card tables as normal young men, but by the time they ended up at her door they were all the same, looking like stray dogs, smelling like garbage trucks and acting like Tarzan.

The tires squealed as the convertible roared by. Clearly Tommy-Roy-Bob was furious. The news would be all over Georgetown by midnight that Darcy Skyler was crazy, a gun-toting man hater. Good. Maybe they'd stop bothering her, at least for a while.

But even a gun wouldn't keep them away forever, if George didn't stop his foolishness. She had no illusions about what lured all these lusty young men to her door. She knew they had been sitting at George's poker table for hours, guzzling his scotch and drinking in his stories of his beautiful stepdaughter and of the fortune he controlled for her.

Mostly it was just braggadocio, but sometimes, on very rare and horrible occasions, he even put the key to their house up as his ante. And if he lost—which, thank God, he rarely did—the winner could use the key and try his luck with the beautiful stepdaughter.

The boys must have been furious when they realized the stepdaughter wasn't a willing participant in the game. She often wondered what they told George the next time he dropped the key on the table. But, knowing George, it probably didn't bother him. He had humiliated her, and that was enough.

Eyeing herself in the tall foyer mirrors opposite, she couldn't help seeing the irony of it all. Beautiful? Hardly. The Tommy-Roy-Bobs were always shocked to discover that George's "princess" was merely a quite average twenty-two-year-old woman. Brown hair, thick and glossy, but nothing spectacular. Large brown eyes, warm when they smiled, but hardly the eyes of an enchantress.

She wiped her brow with the hand that still held the gun. Brown-on-brown—it sounded like a police bulletin. White woman, twenty-two, one hundred and five pounds, brown on brown. It could describe any one of a million women here in the Washington area alone.

But the money was real . . .

Darcy slowly latched the door and twisted the dead bolt, suddenly exhausted. She might as well turn in. Mrs. Christopher wasn't coming back. Thursday was her night with her married daughter in Arlington. That was why Thursdays were the worst for this kind of thing. George undoubtedly slipped that into the conversation early...the housekeeper's night out...the young stepdaughter alone, lonely...

Oh, George, you fool. But she was too tired to work up her usual fury. Sighing, she flipped off a wall switch, and the light melted out of the huge carriage lamp that hung from the two-story foyer ceiling. As if on cue, moonbeams poured through the fanlight over the front doors, lighting her way up the wide stairs.

She moved slowly, past the landing with its table of night-blackened roses, and up toward the long, dark hall of the second floor. The gun cast an elongated shadow on the pale green carpet.

As she did every night, even when she was worn out, she paused at Tessa's door.

"Are you awake?" Darcy whispered, hoping she'd get no response. The crack under the door was black. Good. At only fifteen, Tessa had witnessed too many of these scenes already. Just to be sure, though, she eased the door open.

"Tessa Skyler, what do you think you're doing?"

The dark blob that had been huddled near the window started and jumped down.

"Darcy! I was just watching—" The form took shape. In the moonlight, Tessa's red hair looked brown, and her white T-shirt, which barely covered the lace of her bikinis, seemed a dirty gray.

But then Darcy flicked on the overhead light, and the colors sprang to life. Tessa's green eyes were wide, sparkling, her tousled hair flaming. No brown-on-brown for this younger Skyler princess. Tessa was red-on-green, like roses on the vine, like Christmas trees, like stoplights. In spite of her annoyance, Darcy smiled. Poised on the edge of womanhood, Tessa was gorgeous. Just wait until the poker players discovered her....

Never! Darcy bit her lip hard, the smile dying. She'd never let them get to Tessa. She'd protected her little sister ever since their father died, and she would continue to protect her. But even as she said them to herself, the brave words sounded hollow. Protect her? How? Tessa became more beautiful every day...and harder to control...

Anxiety twisted at Darcy's heart, and she spoke more sharply than she had intended.

"Go back to bed, Tessa. The peep show is over."

Undaunted, Tessa bounced on the bed, crossing her impossibly long legs under her. "I wasn't *peeping* Darcy. I was just watching. I saw you going down with George's starter pistol, and I couldn't help wondering what you were going to do with it. Wow! You were wonderful!"

Darcy grinned in spite of herself. She hadn't been *wonderful* exactly, but she had managed to fool tonight's Romeo fairly successfully. She held the pistol up and studied it.

"If he'd been any less pie-eyed, he'd have known it wasn't real," she decided. "I was just lucky."

"He was kind of drunk, wasn't he?" Tessa nibbled her fingernail, then, realizing what she was doing, tucked the hand inside her knee. "But he was so cute."

Darcy frowned. "Cute?"

"Yeah. I've seen him before, at the club. Everybody thinks he's a hunk." Tessa's green eyes grew dreamy, and she plopped herself back against the pillows, her tanned legs dark against the white linen. "I wish he'd been looking for me! I wouldn't have threatened to shoot him, that's for sure."

"Is that so?" Darcy tried to make her voice playful, tried not to sound judgmental. She remembered well how she, at fifteen, had hated parental inquisitions. "What would you have done?"

Tessa let her eyes roll shut in imaginary ecstasy. "Invited him in, of course." She hugged her pillow hard. "Ummm . . . and then maybe we'd dance in front of the fire."

Darcy couldn't help smiling. Had she ever been that young? It was a dim, sepia memory, but yes, she probably had been. Way back—before stepfathers one, two and three. Before the poker boys at midnight. Before George.

The smile faded. "I don't think he came for a dance, Tessa," she said dryly and snapped off the overhead light. "But let's just forget him. I want you to get to sleep. It's tomorrow already."

She shut the door on Tessa's protests and made her way slowly toward her room. Tessa was so lovely, so naively romantic. George and his poker boys would soon be circling like vultures. Something would have to be done. But what? She wouldn't inherit her money for another three years, and if she tried to take Tessa away without George's permission... She scrunched her eyes, blotting out the thoughts. She was too tired to decide tonight.

She was only halfway down the long hall when she heard the noises downstairs. A metallic scrape of glass against silver, a low curse. Her chest constricted. George.

She gripped the polished wood of the banister tightly, and summoning all her energy, she turned back down the moonlit stairs.

"I threw it away, George," she called out defiantly. Why, even now that she was twenty-two years old, did a confrontation with George still frighten her? Her mother had been dead for three years, and for those three years she had taken care of Tessa and herself just fine, though George's drinking had grown worse with every passing month.

Even so, her heart was bumping idiotically in her breast as her feet numbly followed the curving steps. "I had Mrs. Christopher dump every bottle in the house."

She hesitated at the foot of the stairs, clutching the newel post with both white hands. No noise, no angry outburst. She had been braced for his rage, and the silence was disconcerting. The library was still dark, though she knew he was in there, probably hunched over the liquor cabinet, his anger growing every moment. . . .

A shuffling sound. Her shoulders tightened defensively, but instead of the outraged roar she had expected, the sound that met her ears was more like a soft tittering—or a giggle. A giggle?

Suddenly two figures were outlined in the library doorway, leaning so close together they seemed to be holding each other up. George's broad shoulders, the ex-football player's pride, carefully maintained three times a week at the gym, were unmistakable. How ridiculous to have a stepfather who wasn't yet forty! Oh, Mother, she said tightly, inwardly. Oh, Mother, what a mess!

She didn't immediately recognize the smaller body next to him, but she recognized the type. Her anxiety turned quickly to anger, and she strode across the foyer to the light switch.

A torrent of light gushed over them, drenching their pink faces, forcing them to squint against it. The young woman, apparently the more sober of the two, collected herself first and smiled slyly.

"Why, she's not your mother, George. She's too young to be your mother," she teased, dropping her blond head against George's wide shoulder. George's girlfriends were always blondes. "But she sure sounds like your mother." She slid red nails inside his lapels. "Have you been a bad boy, George?"

George's handsome face was ruddier than usual, and Darcy's heart sank. She forced herself to meet his bloodshot gaze, knowing his anger, which would be unleashed when they were alone, would be fearsome.

But he wouldn't display it in front of his girlfriend. Men like George never exposed their true natures to the world. They were so suave in public, so tragically different at home. That's how they got away with so much ugliness: no one would believe that good old George was really so cruel.

She watched him swallow the anger, and his blue eyes narrowed as he pulled one corner of his mouth up in a smirk.

"Not old enough?" He draped his arm around the blonde's bare shoulders. "Don't let her looks fool you, Abby. She may look twenty-two, but she's got the heart of an old lady. All dried up and uptight."

Abby giggled again, and with such an appreciative audience, George warmed to his role.

"Yeah, she's decided it's her job to stamp out vice wherever she sees it. A caped crusader, flying around smashing bottles of scotch with her bare hands. Super-spinster, we call her."

Darcy bit her lip, refusing to rise to the bait. Obviously George was in the mood for a brawl. Well, she wouldn't give him the satisfaction. Without meeting his eyes, she turned toward the stairs.

"Good night, George. We'll talk in the morning."

"I won't be here in the morning," he returned smoothly. "It's goodbye, not good-night, princess. I'll be in the Bahamas, where even Mrs. Christopher can't throw away all the Margaritas."

In the Bahamas? As the news sank in, Darcy's feet stopped climbing.

"But you can't. You *have* to be here tomorrow, George," she said slowly, turning back to face him, her face paling. "We have a meeting with the board of directors and the trustees first thing in the morning. Had you forgotten?"

Malicious pleasure distorted his handsome features. "Not forgotten, princess. Canceled." He yawned ostentatiously. "I canceled the meeting. Trustees can wait. Margaritas and marlin can't."

Anger made her incoherent, and she took two steps down toward him. "But George, that meeting is important. We are going to discuss my taking over the buying. Don't you remember that we decided—"

She broke off, appalled by the satisfied smile that had spread George's thin lips wide. George might be a lecher and a drunkard, but he was no fool. She had insulted him, and he had zeroed in on the perfect vengeance: his control over Skyler Stores. For the next three years, or until Darcy married, he had full control of her father's chain of luxury department stores.

Yes, it was perfect, and she had to clamp down the bitterness that rose in her throat. He had known for years that she was vulnerable on only two points—her father's business and her little sister. He had never hesitated to use that knowledge when it served him.

A silent laugh shook his broad shoulders.

"Well, you see, I've changed my mind, princess. You're just not ready to take over the buying. I've decided to promote Josie Wilcox to that position."

Josie Wilcox! Darcy had to press her lips together to keep from scoffing out loud. Josie Wilcox, whose only experience was one year as an assistant buyer and whose only talents were an hourglass figure and a knack for buttering up the boss, would be promoted? Josie, whose idea of a great dress was a little silk and a lot of cleavage, would be the head buyer?

Anger rose in her like a geyser, swift and hot. Skyler Stores, a well-respected chain of upscale department stores along the eastern seaboard, had been the tender creation of her grandfather's industry. It had been her father's joy and life's work. And now it was her legacy. She loved the business as a true Skyler, understood it as a true Skyler.

And yet this man kept her prisoner in the public relations department, where she wasted her days sending out puffy press releases about the new spring lines, and organizing VIP tours for visiting bigwigs. "We've got her in training," George always said with a smile, enjoying his power.

And three years still remained before she could stop him, three years of miserable decisions like this one.

"I think it's a mistake to give Josie that job, George," she said as levelly as she could, forcing her anger back into its hidden compartment. "You'd better reconsider."

His face burned bright red, except for the deep white scar that ran from his eyebrow into his hairline, and she knew he was furious. "*I'd* better reconsider? Oh, no, princess, it's *you* who'd better reconsider. You haven't forgotten who runs Skyler Stores, have you?"

His deep voice boomed as his temper got the better of his careful pose, and Darcy glanced nervously toward the head of the stairs. She didn't want Tessa to wake up.

"Come on, Miss Princess. Answer me." He moved toward the banister, his small blue eyes glittering. "Do I run Skyler Stores or not?"

She lifted her chin, giving him stare for stare. Pride clogged her throat, and she wasn't going to answer him. They both knew the terms of her mother's will, and they both knew how hard she had tried to break it, tried to wrest control from this man who had taken over just because, as the "Last Stepfather," he had inherited control of her trust. The lawyers had been sympathetic, but emphatic. Only time, or marriage, could alter the state of things. No matter how violently Darcy disagreed with George's decisions, until she married or turned twenty-five, George was in full control.

Their gazes remained locked, neither willing to look away first, until the soft voice behind her broke the angry spell.

"Darcy?" Tessa had crept out of her room. "Is everything okay?"

At her sister's soft voice Darcy whipped around, her long hair stinging her neck. Tessa looked anxious and, as her green eyes settled on George's girlfriend, tugged on her T-shirt, vainly trying to stretch it to cover her thighs. "I didn't know we had company," she added awkwardly.

"Everything's fine, Tessa," Darcy said through clenched teeth. Really, Tessa ought to know better than to traipse around half-naked. "But you're supposed to be asleep. Go back to bed."

Tessa's green eyes squinted, etching a faint furrow into her clear brow, and Darcy's annoyance dissipated. Poor Tessa. "Go to bed, sweetheart," she said again, more gently.

Tessa hesitated, looking from Darcy to George and back again. "But . . . aren't you coming, Darcy?"

Darcy smiled. "Sure, honey," she said. "I'm coming. George just wanted to say goodbye. He's going to the Bahamas in the morning."

She shot George a sharp look, warning him not to continue the brawl. But he wasn't looking at her. To her dismay he was looking at Tessa, intently, his mouth slightly slack, his eyes narrowing as they slid up her long legs to her pretty face. Tessa seemed oblivious, but Darcy knew that look, and it made her cold all over.

Instinctively she hurried up to the landing and planted herself in front of her sister, blocking his view. No, she heard her blood saying as it drummed in her temples. No, no, no, no. Not Tessa.

"Well, good-night," Tessa said politely, recovering her poise now that the yelling was over. Tessa was like that: trusting and easily reassured. And George had always been so careful not to show his true colors to Tessa. She knew he had a "grumpy temper," as she put it, but she couldn't even imagine the ugliness that lay behind his smile. "I hope you have a nice trip, George."

"Oh, I will, sweetheart, I will." His gaze moved from Tessa's young body to meet Darcy's flashing brown eyes. He knew how upset she was, she realized, and he was enjoying it. George loved to upset people. It made him feel powerful. "Say—you don't want to come with me, do you, Tessa, honey? This time of year Paradise Island is—'' he grinned ''—well, it's paradise.''

Tessa looked intrigued and sneaked Darcy a questioning look. Darcy slipped her arm around her sister, pressing just tightly enough to communicate her disapproval.

''No. Tessa needs to stay here.''

''Why?'' George winked at Tessa. ''We could have some fun together, couldn't we, sweetheart? We could fish . . . and things.''

A cold knot lay at the pit of Darcy's stomach. So this was it. This was the day she had dreaded all these years, the day when Tessa was old enough to interest George in *that* way. Memories stampeded toward her, old memories, but cruelly clear, perfectly preserved. Memories of George, red-eyed, moving inexorably closer. Memories of the broken beer bottle that lay on the floor between them. The one moment of panic, of lashing out, and then memories of the blood that streamed from the gash in his temple, of the fury in his eyes as he backed away . . . defeated.

George had never tried to bother her again, obviously recognizing in Darcy a strength and courage beyond her years. But could the same be said of Tessa?

Her arm tightened around her sister. Tessa murmured a surprised protest and wriggled loose. ''Darcy, that hurts!''

Her sister's voice, clear and young, scattered the ugly memories for Darcy like a strong wind. Her mind was blown clean. All that remained was the unshakable resolution that Tessa would never have such memories. Never.

She knew what that meant, what she would have to do. It was a decision that once would have horrified her.

But now she saw it was the only answer, and she was ready to do whatever it took to protect Tessa.

"Sorry, honey," Darcy said, affixing a smile to her frozen lips. They had to get back to their rooms somehow, without arousing George's suspicions. If he knew what she had decided...

"I'm just pooped. We'd better turn in. Tess, Mrs. Christopher didn't change my linen today. Do you mind if I sleep in your room tonight?"

Tessa smiled. "No, that's great! C'mon." She took the stairs two at a time, calling back gaily, "'Night, all. Have a good trip."

Darcy forced her numb legs to follow her sister, but over her shoulder she heard George's laughter. It built in volume and in virulence, until it seemed to poison the air around her. Her pace quickened, and she fairly raced down the hall until, with trembling hands, she slammed Tessa's door on the sound.

WHEN THEY REACHED Florida, it had been at dawn, a silver dawn, swabbed randomly with pink sponges.

Only Darcy saw it. Tessa had slept on the plane, just as she now slept soundly beside her in the rental car, as trusting as ever, apparently believing that this whispered flight through the summer night, all the way from Washington, D.C., to Sanibel Island, Florida, made sense, just because Darcy had decreed it.

She hadn't even seriously questioned Darcy's sudden decision to get married.

"Evan?" was all she had said, screwing up her face. Evan wasn't her idea of a hero. And then, "Are you sure? I thought you didn't like Evan that way."

Darcy had explained calmly, making her decision sound purely pragmatic. George was making a mess of their father's business and it was time to stop him. Marriage was the only way.

Tessa knew how much Skyler Stores meant to Darcy, and she had all too often heard her arguing with George about it, so she wasn't taken completely by surprise. And she, who had grown up without a mother, was used to obeying her big sister.

Complaining only once or twice that it didn't sound very romantic, she soon entered into the spirit of the clandestine adventure, admitting that she'd be glad not to have to live with George anymore. "He drinks too much these days, and it makes him really obnoxious."

Darcy had laughed, coming dangerously close to hysteria at Tessa's innocent understatement. But, controlling her voice, she had quietly agreed.

Darcy wished that she could be as certain as she sounded. She eased her foot off the gas, in no hurry to reach her destination. The water that lay before her was a wide swath of spangled silk, torn in half by the white ribbon of causeway. So beautiful, and yet . . . Was she crazy to have flown all the way to Florida without calling first? Evan had promised he would always be there for her, but it had been almost six months since his last letter . . .

She pulled the car to the side of the causeway near some picnic tables and unfolded Evan's most recent letter one more time. She always kept it with her, her secret talisman.

He wanted her to know he still loved her, still hoped someday to marry her. If ever she needed him, he said, she should just come to him. He would be waiting.

It was the same promise he'd made her accept on graduation day. A pact, he had called it. She had protested. It wasn't necessary, she had said. But he had insisted. And thank heaven, thank heaven he had.

But what on earth was she going to say? She hadn't ever told him the truth about George. He knew she despised her stepfather. He knew she hated watching him run Skyler Stores. But he didn't know about that horrible day when George had tried... No one knew. Her mother had been alive then, and even she hadn't believed her. After that Darcy hadn't had the courage to tell anyone else, not even the police. Would they have believed her, a hysterical sixteen-year-old, against a well-respected businessman? And besides, she'd felt irrationally ashamed, guilty, frightened...

But she couldn't think about that right now. She had to find Evan. The return address on the letter was Two Palms, Gull Terrace, Sanibel Island, so she steered the car back onto the causeway and entered the island proper, checking street signs.

Gull Terrace wasn't far, and within minutes she spotted a small blue sign peeking from a thick bouquet of periwinkles: Two Palms. She let the car idle, studying the property, stalling as she tried to inflate her flattened courage. The house was two stories high, painted as yellow as the morning sun, with shutters as white as the sand. The Gulf shimmered behind it, like a vat of green sequins. And on either side of the long white porch, two towering royal palms lifted their crowns to the clouds.

Finally her heart lightened. It was a good house, simple and welcoming, like Evan himself. Deciding not to wake Tessa, she clambered out of the car, her feet almost silent as she traversed the soft layer of pine needles and took the steps to the front door.

She knocked several times, and the sound echoed hollowly. The long silence worried her. Wasn't he here?

"Can I help you?"

The voice came from behind her, and she whirled, startled.

"Oh, I'm sorry," she stammered, disoriented by the sight of this stranger, obviously risen from an early-morning swim in the Gulf. His legs were still wet, glistening. "I'm looking for Mr. Hawthorne."

The man before her squinted into the sun. Flicking down the towel that lay over his bronzed shoulders, he used it to push back the dark, wet curls that were dangling over his wide brow and dripping onto his impossibly long lashes. And then he squinted at her again.

"I'm sorry...have we met?"

She shook her head. She most definitely did not know this man. She had never known a man so extravagantly masculine. His swimming trunks—if such an old-fashioned phrase could be used to describe anything as brief as this molded piece of cloth—revealed a body so lean and tanned, so perfectly formed that it almost didn't look real. He might have been one of the mannequins in Skyler Stores...except for the way he was making her feel. No mannequin could have brought the blood to her cheeks like this....

"No," she said, shaking her head. "No, I don't think so. I'm Darcy Skyler. I'm looking for Evan Hawthorne."

The man slipped the white towel behind his neck and held the edges with both hands. His eyes widened, just long enough for her to glimpse their bottomless brown, and then narrowed again. The dark brows contracted.

"Ah...Darcy Skyler." He seemed to know the name, but he didn't smile. The square jaw tightened. "Well,

let me welcome you to Two Palms, Darcy, since my
brother isn't here to do it. He's in the middle of the Atlantic right now, delivering a boat to one of our clients
in the Bahamas. But perhaps I can help you . . . I'm his
brother, Miles.''

CHAPTER TWO

HER FIRST REACTION was that it wasn't possible.

She had known, of course, that Evan had an older brother. But this man didn't look anything like an older version of Evan. This man, this Miles Hawthorne, was so...so potent. So male. So at home here in the elements, with the salty water drying on his maple skin, his long, delineated muscles still dusted with sand.

And he was too young, surely? No more than thirty-one or two. Struggling to remember what Evan had said about him, she stared stupidly at the diamondlike drops winking on his broad chest. Big brother Miles, the family patriarch, Miles the obsessive businessman, Miles the benevolent despot. The details were fuzzy, but a mental picture of a stodgy, horn-rimmed type had formed and stuck. Evan had never, never implied such a devastating virility...

But then Miles's words sank in, and her second reaction was undiluted panic. Evan wasn't here. Evan was out on a boat, unreachable, unable to help her. Dismay was like an anchor, and her heart plummeted.

"Are you all right?"

Miles stepped closer, his narrowed brown eyes hard on her. Her sinking heart had dragged the blood out of her face, and she knew she must be pale. She tried for a smile, but it felt shaky.

"I'm fine," she lied. "I was just hoping to see Evan." She reached back and braced herself against the porch railing. "I needed to talk to him..."

Her voice melted away. She couldn't explain to this hard-featured brother why she needed to talk to Evan.

"Well, you can't," he said after a long pause in which his assessing gaze seemed to see it all—the pallor, the panic, the false bravado—and find it boring. "It'll be days before he makes land. And he's taking a short vacation after the delivery. He might call in, but there's no telling when. A week or two, I'd think, at the least."

Two weeks! Her lips fell open, and she reached a trembling hand up to touch her numb cheek. No Evan, no raft to cling to in the sudden turbulence of her life. She made a small choking sound. Now what would she do?

"But, on his vacation—he must have told you where he would be staying," she said, hoping she didn't sound as desperate as she felt.

"No." His tone was uncompromising. "He's a big boy. He doesn't have to file a travel plan with me."

She swallowed and brought her gaze back to his. The look in his dark eyes surprised her. He looked angry...very. But at whom? Surely not at her. She couldn't have made any heinous mistakes in a two-minute acquaintance.

Yet something unpleasant lurked behind those eyes. And unless she had gone completely crazy, he was downright *glad* that she had missed Evan. She frowned instinctively. Why?

His gaze caught the frown, and again she got the impression her discomfort pleased him.

"Apparently he doesn't file his travel plans with you anymore, either," he said with a lazy and not altogether pleasant smile. "You look shocked. Are you so accustomed to having Evan at your fingertips?"

She shook her head, bewildered by the caustic tone. "Of course not. I had just hoped . . . I just wanted . . ."

"Wanted what? For him to sit around and wait, on the off chance that you'd decide to visit?"

She swallowed again and slanted another look at him. His eyes were hard, black, his mouth tight.

"Of course not. Just to see him," she said, her voice stiff with indignation and confusion.

"Well, you can see him in a couple of weeks. This time it'll take more than the snapping of your fingers to bring him running. He can't hear snapping all the way across the Atlantic."

She squinted, unaccountably hurt by his snide tone, though it was now clear why Miles disliked her. Evan must have confided in his big brother, must have reported that Darcy had turned down his frequent proposals. *Protective,* Evan had said of his brother. Well, that was certainly an understatement!

Suddenly tears were humiliatingly close to the surface. Damn his nasty, belligerent attitude. She wasn't a weeper. She was tough, strong, determined. How ridiculous that she, who had never cried in the face of George's cruelties, should be choked with tears at this man's rudeness.

She turned away, wishing his nasty comments didn't sting so sharply. After all, her relationship with Evan was none of his business. He had no right to judge her.

But she turned too quickly, stumbling as unshed tears warped her vision and caused her to trip on the stairs. He caught her elbow roughly, almost unwillingly, and steadied her.

"Careful," he growled. And perhaps he felt the trembling in her arm, for he pressed hard, pushing her toward the steps. "Sit."

She resisted, but his hand was strong, and soon her wobbling knees gave way and she sank to a seat on the top step. He watched her for a minute, scowling. "It must have been pretty urgent," he said finally. "What's going on?"

She didn't answer. He didn't deserve an answer. She tried to concentrate on recovering her equilibrium, but it was as elusive as smoke. She really was so tired.

In spite of her spurt of anger, all the strength she had marshaled to see her through last night's desperate decision was depleted now. She had been holding herself together for the past exhausted hours with a kind of bitter pride. And she had just about run out of that, too.

After a moment he squatted in front of her, his hands dangling between his bare knees. The bathing suit he wore hid nothing, not even the tight hollows below the ridge of his hipbones, and yet he held that pose with a superb confidence, as though armed with a designer suit and tie.

A hot tear trickled down her cheek, its salty warmth pooling around the edges of her lips. It tasted the way the Florida air smelled. Before she could brush it away, he reached out, rubbed lightly at the moistness and then tucked his wet fingertips under her chin.

"Maybe I can find him," he said slowly, as though the words spoke themselves, without his permission. "Where are you staying?"

She opened her mouth to answer, though she didn't know what she would say. She had been counting on staying here, at Two Palms, with Evan. But another voice broke the awkward silence.

"Hey, you guys, it's getting hot out here. And besides, I'm about to starve to death!"

Tessa! Darcy realized she had almost forgotten poor Tessa, whom she had left sleeping in the car. She came toward them now, a vision even in her cut-off blue jeans and green T-shirt, a mischievous grin on her pretty face. She had hoisted her duffel bag over one shoulder, and her makeup case dangled from the other hand.

"Hi, Evan," she said, as Miles rose slowly to his feet, the dark look returning, suggesting he already regretted his moment of near kindness. "I'm Tessa. Darcy sure was eager to see you. She wouldn't even stop to get us breakfast."

Darcy rose, too, embarrassment forcing strength into her legs. Unaware of her blunder, Tessa was giving Miles an uninhibited once-over, from the still-damp dark curls to the sand-sprinkled bare toes. And she was clearly admiring what she saw. She turned to Darcy, her grin deepening, a gleam in her eyes.

"Tessa," Darcy said quellingly, hoping to nip any indiscreet comments in the bud. "This is Miles. He's Evan's brother. Evan isn't here."

"Oh." Tessa looked disappointed. Then she frowned. "Evan's not here?" She looked longingly toward the cool house, and back at the car, which sat baking under the rising sun. Her momentary high spirits had floated away, and she was just a fussy, tired fifteen-year-old kid who badly wanted some pancakes and a nap. "I told you we should have called. Now where will we stay? I'm tired, Darcy."

The plaintive note tugged at Darcy's heart.

"We'll find something, sweetheart," she said sooth-ingly. "Sanibel must have dozens of cottages—"

"But you'd obviously planned to stay here, hadn't you?" Miles's voice was not quite rude, apparently in deference to Tessa, but Darcy heard the sarcasm un-derneath the civility. "You were very sure of your wel-come."

Tessa smiled. "Oh, yes," she said. "Darcy and Evan are very close. Very." She emphasized the word dra-matically, delighted with her secret. "He must have told you about Darcy."

"Of course," he replied smoothly, flicking Darcy a glance that managed in a split second to be profoundly insulting. "I know all about Darcy."

"Well, then can't we just wait here for him?" Tessa looked at Miles, dimpling. "We're pooped. I didn't sleep all night."

She had, of course. She had slept on the plane and again in the car. But Darcy didn't bother to correct her.

"Evan won't be back for a couple of weeks. We'll find a cottage," Darcy said again, more firmly, and took the duffel bag from Tessa. She didn't look at Miles. "We'll let you know where we're staying, and if you'll just tell Evan to call me..."

"No." The syllable was as final as the closing of a door. She glanced at Miles, surprised.

"If you're planning to stay on the island, waiting for him, you'll say here," he said, striding over and whisk-ing the duffel bag out of her loose grip. "Evan would want you to."

"No..." But her own syllable lacked the force of his. She heard her confusion in the weak and faltering word.

"Oh, Darcy, please. *Please?*" Tessa's voice was again plaintive, and her touch on Darcy's arm was urgent.

She'd never found it easy to deny Tessa anything, especially when she sounded so pitiful. At a loss, Darcy fell back on meaningless civility. "Tessa, we don't want to impose."

"Nonsense." Mile's strong hand took her other arm. "It wouldn't be an imposition—not when you and Evan are so *very* close."

Recognizing an ally, Tessa squeaked with glee. And with one of them on either side of her, pushing, imploring, insisting, Darcy was led up the stairs.

Without letting go of her, Miles swung open the door, revealing an airy, sunlit room beyond. It ran the breadth of the house, and the far wall was entirely plate glass windows, giving a panoramic view of the Gulf and the blue morning sky.

As Darcy watched helplessly, Tessa gasped and ran to admire the sparkling water.

"Oh, Darcy, isn't it terrific?" She slid open the glass doors and stepped outside, calling over her shoulder in breathless happiness, "I just love the beach."

Miles stood back, watching her from eyes that were almost black. "Think of it as a vacation, compliments of your close friend Evan," he said, in tones so low that Tessa couldn't hear him, tones that still managed to convey limitless sarcasm. He watched Tessa rush to the railing, laughing.

"But don't let her love it too much," he added tightly. "You may not be staying as long as you think."

THE HOT RED SUN had already dipped its rim in the Gulf and was about to sizzle out, but still Darcy sat on the porch outside her bedroom, watching the sky.

She ought to go down. She had slept most of the day, but an hour ago Miles had sent up the message that he'd like her to join him for dinner at nine.

Clearly nervous, Tessa had pleaded exhaustion and was even now tucked into the big double bed in her own guest room, leaning against a silk backrest, watching television and eating dinner served on a silver tray.

Darcy would have liked to do the same, but she refused to let Miles think he'd intimidated her. So she had showered and rummaged through her hastily packed suitcase for something to wear.

Nothing seemed right. Oddly the things she'd packed to wear with Evan suddenly wouldn't do. After one short meeting, she knew Miles Hawthorne would be more difficult to impress. She settled for a silk skirt and blouse the color of wood violets, the dressiest thing she had brought. She pulled her long brown hair back in a low ponytail and then wound a blue ribbon around it, leaving just a flash of hair free at the end.

It would have to do. But still she dawdled on the wide white porch, as cowardly as Tessa, reluctant to confront him. She had no doubt that *confront* was the right word. This morning she had been too tired to think clearly, and disappointment and shame had been her dominant emotions. Tonight, though, anger had risen to the top. Miles Hawthorne was a mannerless boor, and he had made it clear that he despised her. He clearly saw himself as king of the mountain, and he probably expected her to come downstairs tonight, groveling, wilted and afraid, and eager to make amends.

Well, he might be king, but it was Evan's house, too, and Evan would never expect her to grovel. She lifted her chin and bit her lips together. It would be awkward to have a brother-in-law who despised her, but she could stand it. If Evan would just hurry up and call....

But it must be after nine already. The beach was almost empty, except for the small birds that skittered back and forth, following some unseen maze along the shore. Only one couple remained in the twilight. They had stood there a long time, deep in conversation, and they probably didn't even realize the sun had already drowned in the purpling Gulf.

Darcy hadn't meant to stare, but when the woman suddenly wrenched away from the man, the abrupt movement startled her. The woman, a lithe young blonde, called out an angry sentence that the wind swept away, and then hurled herself off down the beach, scattering seabirds as she ran. A lover's spat, Darcy thought, smiling to herself. But in such a beautiful setting as this, surely they couldn't stay angry long.

Something unfamiliar stirred in the pit of her stomach as she contemplated the man. Yes, he looked like a man who could not easily be rejected. They would probably be back in each other's arms by moonlight. She crossed her arms over her chest as the breeze picked up and caused her to shiver. Together, and in love—but she, Darcy, would still be alone. Irrationally her throat felt thick and stiff. She would marry Evan, whom she didn't love, and in some profound way she would always be alone.

Oh, she definitely should go in. She was starting to sound maudlin and was dangerously close to feeling sorry for herself. These were childish thoughts. She had made her decision, and she would live by it. She would be a good wife to Evan, and he would never regret marrying her.

She stood up and had almost turned to go when her gaze caught the man who had been left behind on the beach. He still stared toward where the woman had run, and his profile was etched boldly and blackly against the purple sky. Darcy's heart skittered like the birds she had been watching. It was Miles.

Against her will she walked to the railing and stared down at him. Dressed in white shorts and a long-sleeved white cotton shirt, he gleamed, the one bright spot in the darkening twilight. The evening breeze blew from behind him, molding his clothes against the lean contours of his body, and she was struck again with the pure masculinity of his form. His dark hair, now dry, was thick and loosely curled, and the wind tickled it against his ears.

He was clearly lost in his own thoughts, his hands jammed into his pockets and his eyes fixed on some spot far down the beach. Darcy wondered what they had quarreled about. What could have made the lovely blonde tear herself from under his protecting arm and leave him stranded here?

With a soft crunch of sand Miles whirled suddenly and strode toward the house. Embarrassed, though he probably couldn't see her, Darcy darted back into the shadows of the porch. The blonde was no business of hers, and she was inexcusably late for dinner.

"SLEEP WELL?"

He was waiting, as poised and unruffled as if he had never been standing in the night wind. The blonde and her angry departure might have been a figment of Darcy's imagination.

She nodded warily. "Very, thank you. We were really awfully tired. We had been on the plane all night."

"So I gathered." One dark brow went up, but he didn't question her further, simply motioning her in to where the table was already set for two.

The first part of the dinner passed in silence, with Alice, the pretty maid, bringing in the clam chowder and then taking away Miles's empty bowl and Darcy's nearly full one equally without comment.

As Alice served the main course, a delicately broiled flounder, Darcy began to wonder why Miles had invited her to dinner at all, as he clearly didn't enjoy her company. Trying to unnerve her, perhaps? A bit of the silent treatment, hoping to freeze her out? Well, it wouldn't work. She speared a bite of flounder, settled a polite smile on her lips and prepared to outlast him.

As though he sensed her decision and the failure of his plan, he spoke. "There's a tropical storm brewing in the Caribbean. If it heads this way, Evan may have to cut his vacation short."

She swallowed her fish without tasting it. "Oh, no. Is there any danger?" Her mouth was dry, and she took a sip of wine. "While he's on the boat, I mean. Could the storm bother him?"

He chewed slowly, his gaze on her and a small, unpleasant smile at the corners of his lips. "Worried about Evan, Darcy? That's very touching."

She squeezed her napkin and clenched her teeth. He was just trying to get a rise out of her, and she mustn't cooperate. "Well? Could it?"

He put his fork down and leaned back in his chair. "Of course not. Do you think I would even have allowed him to start out if there had been any danger? You underestimate me, Darcy. I take my job as a big brother very seriously."

"Really? What exactly is a big brother's job?" His implication had been obvious, and her cheeks were hot, but she met his gaze steadily.

"Simple, really." He smiled that half smile she was rapidly learning to hate. "It's not unlike sailing. Know where the rocks and shallows are, know when the squalls are coming, and steer the boat away from them into safer water."

In spite of her irritation at his smug tone, she knew what he meant. It was a pretty good description of a big sister's job, too. Maybe he wasn't so unreasonable after all. If someone had hurt Tessa, she might be just as angry as he was now.

"Unfortunately, sometimes the boat balks," he went on, his voice glassy. "Sometimes it seems to have a mind of its own. It almost seems to *want* to go into the rocks. Then you really have to get tough."

She narrowed her eyes at the direct hit. Did he think she was too stupid to understand the unspoken message—or was he *trying* to insult her?

"Listen, Miles," she began, dropping her fork with a clatter, but he cut her off smoothly.

"Of course, on this trip Evan's sailing the *Miranda*. She's a sweet handler. He should be fine."

He had gone back to his fish, as though the earlier exchange had really been only about boats. Okay, she said silently. We'll forget that one. Restraint, Darcy, she told herself, and jammed her fork back into her flounder.

"The *Miranda?*" she asked politely, though she had to pry her teeth apart to speak. "Is that one of your boats?"

"Ummm," he nodded, still carving his fish. "Hasn't Evan ever mentioned the *Miranda?*"

She shook her head.

"I'm surprised. The Miranda-style boat is one of our best. My father designed the original—a twenty-seven-footer, self-tacking jib, fully battened main, a real beauty. Hawthorne Industries hasn't made a boat like the *Miranda* in twenty years."

"Why not, if it's such a good boat?"

"Good question." He downed the rest of his wine and leaned back. "It was a dumb decision, based on emotion instead of good business sense. My father designed her for my mother, whose name was Miranda. And then when my mother left him, he refused to make any more, threw away the plans. We'd been looking for them since he died ten years ago, and we finally found them. We just started building copies last year."

His indifference shocked her somehow. She'd never heard anyone speak of such a huge trauma with such inhuman calm.

"Your mother left? Why—" she stopped herself midsentence, knowing she had no right to ask such a thing. "Where—where did she go?" she amended quickly.

"New York." Again that blasé tone. "She had been a model before they married, and the life of a boat builder's wife bored her. Sanibel bored her. Children bored her."

She squinted. The sentiments he expressed were so bleak, and yet he sounded so unmoved. "But Hawthorne Industries is a big company. Surely there were opportunities..."

"It wasn't then." He picked up his fork and tapped it end over end on the tablecloth, the only sign of emotion she could detect. "We didn't have any of the yards up the coast, just the little one here. Anyhow, when she left, my father just fell apart. He muddled on for about ten years, but his heart wasn't in it. Finally he died, still grieving.''

At long last she heard something, a note of real pity buried under all that disapproval. It must have been hard, watching his father slowly die of a broken heart.

"I'm sorry," she said quietly. And she was. Her own circumstances had been different, but they had been just as difficult. She would have liked to tell him that she understood lonely childhoods, that she knew how awesome the task of parenting a younger sibling could be. But his manner didn't invite sympathy, and she didn't speak.

"But enough about that." He stood up. "Let's go outside. You and I have some things to straighten out."

She didn't know how he managed to imbue such civilized words with such a sense of danger, but she had to work to keep the Haviland cup from rattling in its saucer as she followed him across the polished wood floors toward the glass doors.

He placed two woven deck chairs near the railing and motioned her to take her place next to him. Balancing his cup on the railing, he leaned back, put his feet up and finally spoke.

"So. What do you want?"

No more pussyfooting, then. Right to the point. Her throat was dry again, and she looked out toward the Gulf, where the full moon floated like a pale balloon over the silver water. She didn't want to meet the gaze she felt he had turned on her. His eyes were too probing.

"What makes you think I want anything?"

"Oh, for God's sake. I'm not a fool," he countered tersely. "Why else would you be here?"

It took her a moment to swallow her indignation at his brutal tone. Getting into a brawl with Evan's brother wasn't any way to start a relationship. But it wasn't easy. He was clearly spoiling for a fight.

In the silence, the tinny music of the crickets and the sandy hiss of the waves seemed abnormally loud. She took another sip of coffee, and even the sound of her swallowing seemed to echo in the night air.

"Well, you see," she began, cursing herself for being a nervous ninny. Perhaps she just ought to tell him to mind his own business. But his manner was so authoritative, as though he never considered defiance a possibility. "Evan and I were very good friends during college. We, well, maybe he has mentioned me..."

"Often." He was still looking steadily at her, but his tone of voice was not revealing. It could have hidden any number of emotions.

"Well," she repeated, and angrily swore she'd never use the stupid word again. "Evan and I talked sometimes about the possibility of our getting married someday. Did you know that?" Oh, this was so hard! Why didn't he say something—anything to help her out of this mess?

But when he spoke, it didn't help at all.

"I know that *he* talked about it. You, as I recall, simply said no thanks, I can do better."

Stunned by the bitterness in his words she stared through the darkness, trying to read his face. But even the full moon didn't shed enough light, and she searched frantically for a response. "That's not true. I never said—"

"So what happened?" he interrupted harshly. "What are you doing here now, after all this time? Did you finally realize you *can't* do better?"

"No," she blurted. "I mean, yes. I mean, that's a damned insulting question." She stood up jerkily, spilling a few drops of hot coffee onto her forearm, and walked across the porch toward the corner of the house.

He didn't follow her. She rested her elbows on the railing, trying to calm herself. She didn't *have* to explain any of this to him. It was ultimately an issue between Evan and herself. Perhaps she should just suggest that Miles go out and find his blonde, and work out his *own* problems...

"Insulting? Oh, that was nothing, Darcy. I have one that's much more insulting than that." She heard him swing his feet down, stand up and walk slowly to where she stood.

She wheeled around to meet him, leaning against the wooden railing, her ponytail swaying out behind her. Anger was clearly in his voice now, and his very presence exuded a faint sense of menace.

"Did it ever occur to you," he said, enunciating every word distinctly, "that *he* could do better than *you?*"

Her skin prickled as indignation shot hot blood to her cheeks.

"Isn't that for him to decide?" She tried to sound strong and calm, but her heartbeat seemed to make her voice flutter.

"No," he said, leaning even closer, until she could see the moon reflected in his black eyes. "He hasn't ever thought very clearly when it came to you. So I've decided for him. He'll never marry you."

"Why not?" Her voice was thin, her lungs tight from the pressure of the railing at her back.

"For starters, because you don't give a damn about him."

She stared at him, her blood rising higher. "What?" How dare he take this tone with her? "I'm very fond of Evan."

"Fond?" He snorted. "That's a laugh."

The rudeness of him baffled her. "What does that mean?"

"It means," he said slowly, "that no one needs a 'fond' wife. Evan deserves better than that." He narrowed his eyes to hard points that seemed to bore into her. "Evan deserves to marry a woman who adores him."

"I do."

"Rot." The syllable exploded from him, and she backed away, the hard wood of the balcony creaking under the pressure of her spine. Contempt was in the set of his lips, the squint of his eyes, the posture of his hard body, and for a craven moment she wanted to flee. But she couldn't run, even if she wanted to; he impaled her with his dark eyes. "You're not half good enough for Evan. Your sickly 'fondness' isn't good enough for him. Why the hell have you come here now, when I thought he might finally be getting over you?"

The railing seemed to shift beneath her hands as the blood ran out of her face. But Miles's hard voice went on and on.

"Evan's been breaking his heart over you for years. And you've given him nothing but grief. He doesn't need you, Darcy Skyler. You're trouble." He reached forward and took hold of her arm.

She wriggled under his grasp. "I never broke Evan's heart," she defended herself hotly, hoping it was true. It *was* true. Evan had always seemed to take her rejections rather well... "And besides, whether he needs me is for Evan himself to decide," she continued, furious. "He—he—"

"No. *He* doesn't need *you*." Miles didn't skip a beat, as though she hadn't spoken at all. "But clearly *you* need *him*. And it must be something pretty important to send you flying down here in the middle of the night." He yanked her closer, his hands stiff with anger, and searched her face with his dark eyes. "What is it? Is it George?"

Her wriggling stopped as if his words had frozen her. George? At first her lips felt too slack to speak, but she bit them together hard and found her voice. "What do you know about George?"

"Everything," he said, and the black word was loaded with implication. "You see, I've known George for years. I went to college with him."

She frowned, stunned by the revelation. But as her mind recovered from the shock, she realized it made a kind of sense. Miles wasn't that much younger than George—only five or six years. Evan had gone to college in Washington, so presumably Miles had done the same, and George, getting to the university late, after military service, had played football there some years back.

But Miles just didn't seem George's type, somehow. Miles was all the things George only wished he was—masculine, powerful, intimidating...

"What does George have to do with me and Evan?" Dammit, this wasn't any of his business. She didn't have to bare her soul, her sad life story, for him. But she wasn't a very good liar, and she tried to turn her head away to hide her discomfort.

He refused to let her escape. "Don't play games with me, Darcy. I told you. I *know* George. I know he talks about you. I know he plays poker with playboys, and your name is bandied about like a soccer ball.

"I even know—" his voice dipped lower "—that sometimes, when he runs out of chips, he puts your house key up as his ante. And the chance to win the favors of his beautiful stepdaughter. He always calls it that—your 'favors'—and he thinks it's very amusing."

Tears welled up in her eyes, and she ducked her head. Oh, God. No wonder Miles thought so little of her. Even Evan didn't know about the poker games.

"How did you know that? How?" Her voice was trembling with the effort to sound normal, and her shoulders were trembling with the effort to stand calmly, the effort to keep from running away into the black night.

"I know," he said, low and hard, "because one night, a few years back, when my luck was particularly good, I won you myself."

CHAPTER THREE

SHE WAS too shocked even to try to pull away. For a dizzied moment it felt as if his hands were actually propping her up as her mind frantically searched back through the leering, drunken faces. Was it possible that this dark, strong face before her now had been one of *them?*

She couldn't believe it, and she felt her head shaking in an instinctive rejection. She knew, somehow, that she would have remembered this man. He was so different from all the others, from the Tommy-Roy-Bobs who had made her skin crawl with their wet-lipped demands and their clammy, groping hands. It even flashed shockingly across her mind that if this man had come, it would have been more difficult to throw him out....

"No," she whispered, frowning from the effort to recall. "No. You weren't one of them..."

Abruptly he let go, and she struggled to find her balance. She groped out behind her, and her fingers clung to the railing.

"No," he agreed. "I wasn't. I just said I won you, not that I ever came to collect my winnings."

Benumbed, she could only watch him blankly, trying to sort it all out, as he moved away. Strange that she had never thought of this possibility before—she had always just written off the poker players as something less than human, not men who might harshly judge her part in George's game.

"Why?"

He leaned over the railing himself and surveyed the wide, calm water before him. His shoulders spread as he shifted his weight onto his hands, and his white shirt stretched across the fabric. The muscles around his shoulder blades were hard and rounded.

"I'm not sure," he said. "Just not quite to my taste, I suppose. Something a little off-putting about winning a woman at poker, don't you think?"

She shook her head, her cheeks burning. "I didn't mean that—"

He turned around. "Oh, I see. You want to know why I was involved in a poker game with the notorious George."

She nodded, and he leaned back against the railing, crossing his arms over his chest and gazing at her speculatively.

"That's a little more complicated," he said. "You see, George and I go way back. We used to play football on the same college team, though he was a senior when I was only a freshman, and we developed a healthy dislike for each other then. But he has some things I want, and I was hoping he'd put them on the table."

He smiled nastily, and his teeth flashed white in the moonlight. "I'm a fairly good poker player, you see, and I knew I could win. But he bet his pretty stepdaughter instead. Apparently that's his favorite party game."

She forced herself to meet his eyes.

"I hope you don't think that I was a willing partici- pant in that insanity," she said, her voice tight. "Or that I ever—"

"I don't know what the hell you are," he inter- rupted. "I only know that somehow you've persuaded Evan that you're George's victim, a damsel in distress. He has quite a Galahad complex about you."

Again she felt her cheeks burning, horrified by the skepticism she heard in his voice. Couldn't he see how mortifying all that had been for her? Couldn't he see past his own cynicism, past the locker room jokes, to the misery of her life?

No, of course he couldn't. He thought of her only as the woman who had hurt his brother, who wanted to hurt him still. And yet surely he could see that she would consider herself lucky if Evan would take her away from George and the sordid life he led.

She opened her mouth to tell him just that, but he was following his own train of thought, and he spoke first.

"He'll get over you, if he gets enough time. You're just a juvenile dream he has. You'd make the kid mis- erable, and we both know it." He ran his hand through his hair roughly, anger and frustration implicit in the motion. "Dammit—I won't let you marry Evan. I don't like George, and I don't like you."

"That's been clear from the outset," she said grimly. "And so?" she prompted. She might as well hear everything. "How do you plan to stop me?"

"I don't think I'll have to bother." He sounded dis- gusted, and rather tired. "I rather think Evan will see through you this time. So stay here. Make yourself at home. But know this, Darcy, and don't forget it. I'm not your friend. I'm sick of you hurting my brother, and I'll stop you if it turns out I have to."

She nodded numbly. "Thank you," she said, screening the sarcasm from her voice, "for the warning."

"Don't thank me," he corrected. "Do Evan harm and you'll have me to answer to. You might wish you had stayed with George."

PREDICTABLY Tessa was delighted. Darcy reported an edited version of her conversation with Miles, but she needn't have been so cautious. Tessa barely listened, hearing only that they could stay before rushing over to dig in her suitcase for a bathing suit.

They spent the entire day on the beach, walking down to Hutto's Market for sandwiches and bringing them back picnic-style to their blankets. The bread got a little sandy and the soft drinks were warm, but Darcy wasn't ready to risk having to eat another meal with Miles.

But by late afternoon, when the handsome young sun worshipers were relinquishing the beach to the more cautious middle-aged set, Tessa grew restless. Darcy had noticed that Two Palms had its own tennis court, so she suggested they play a quick match before the sun went down.

But when they got to the court, which was spread out under a rectangle of palms in the side yard like a pat of smooth green clay, it was already in use. Miles, all bronze and white in regulation tennis wear, was apparently trouncing a younger, but equally bronzed, man who cursed loudly at every point.

Darcy groaned under her breath. Why hadn't she checked first? She put out a hand to halt Tessa's bouncing progress, but she should have known it wouldn't work.

"Hi!" Tessa trilled as the men switched sides between games. "Mind if we watch?"

Both men stopped and looked their way. Lifting her chin, Darcy followed Tessa toward the court. She'd have to see him sooner or later, she told herself. And he might as well discover right now that he hadn't scared her off.

Introductions went around swiftly. Miles's face was expressionless, but the boy, who turned out to be a neighbor named Brad, couldn't take his admiring eyes off Tessa.

"Mind? Not a bit!" Brad was only about eighteen himself, Darcy figured, and he looked nice enough. "In fact, how about a game of doubles? I could use a break. I'm getting my clock cleaned, and Miles hasn't even broken a sweat."

All eyes went automatically to Miles, who was indeed miraculously unruffled, especially compared to his disheveled opponent. The wind had fingered his hair a bit, but it became him, and the light sheen of perspiration made his skin look like wet gold.

"Great!" Tessa slipped on her wristbands, ignoring Darcy's blatant reluctance. "But I'd better be on Miles's team," she lamented. "I'm awful, and it wouldn't be much of a game if he and Darcy teamed up against us."

Brad's face fell, but Darcy could hardly hide her relief. Being Miles's partner would have been a farce, and she doubted whether they could have cooperated well enough to beat even the weakest opponents. But as adversaries—well, that seemed quite natural.

The match started slowly, and Darcy watched with amusement as Brad lobbed one soft ball after another toward Tessa.

Flirtation and good tennis didn't mix. He lost his serve quickly, but he didn't seem to mind a bit. The oh-boy grin never dropped from his lips, and his eyes never left Tessa's face, not even to watch the ball.

But then it was Miles's turn to serve, and the pace changed dramatically. Darcy's breath came harder as she pounded back ball after ball, all of which were aimed at her. Points were long. Miles's control was absolute. He placed the ball neatly in the corners, along the line, always just far enough out of reach to make her scurry and stretch. Sweat broke out along her hairline, and her shoulder began to ache, but she wouldn't give up.

On every point, though, her efforts were in vain. Whenever he tired of tormenting her, he effortlessly delivered an overhead smash so fierce she had no hope of touching it. He won his serve at love and grinned unpleasantly as he tossed the balls to her.

"Nice try." Saccharine sweet.

Irked, she scooped up the balls and made her first serve an ace. His grin froze for an instant and then came back slowly, nastier than ever.

She refused to let it bother her. If this blasted tennis match was to be a metaphor for their personal battles, then he might as well know she still intended to win.

After the first set, which went to Miles and Tessa, Brad called them to the net.

"What do you say you and I bow out, Tessa?" Brad grinned. "Miles and your sister are the ones really playing this match. We're just in the way."

"No—" Darcy began.

"Oh, let the kids go," Miles interrupted. "Brad hates tennis, really. His dad made him promise to play a set every day, like a dose of medicine."

"But Tessa needs—"

"Tessa needs a good walk along the beach," Miles finished for her. "The sun's about to set, and she'll want to see it on the water. Will you take her, Brad?"

"You bet." Brad leaped over the net in one youthful bound, and the two of them hurried away, Tessa casting a half-apologetic, half-impish glance over her shoulder at Darcy.

Darcy watched them go, then turned her furious gaze back to Miles. "Why did you do that?"

"Do what?"

"Take over. Assume control. Horn in."

Miles lifted a tennis ball with the side of his foot, and dribbled it with his racket. "Someone had to. If you wanted control, you should have taken it."

"You didn't give me a chance."

"I don't *give* chances," he said, knocking the balls softly over the net to her court. "If you want to win, you'll have to try harder. Your serve."

He backed away and stood by the baseline, hunkered down, ready to receive and return anything she could send his way.

"I'll do that," she muttered. She tossed a ball up and fired it toward him, her concentration focused with all the pent-up anger she felt. "I'll just do that."

But it was useless. No matter how hard she slammed the balls, no matter how accurately she aimed for the angles, no matter how carefully she plotted her strategy, he was always two steps ahead of her. She couldn't catch him wrong-footed. He seemed to know what she planned before she knew herself.

As the set wore on, her muscles began to burn. Never before had she played an opponent so formidable. Miles made no concessions to her sex. He played all out, and with every whizzing ball she heard the unspoken message—expect no breaks from me. She wiped the sweat away with her wristband and blinked in the growing twilight, trying to catch enough breath to go on. Fair enough. No mercy.

As his lead grew, his shots became, if anything, fiercer. Finally, as exhaustion overtook her, she found herself charging in toward one of his overhead smashes, blindly refusing to accept that it would come in too steep and too fast for her to connect with it.

But she connected all right, though not with her racket. In an explosive moment of heat and pain, the ball slammed against her upper thigh. She managed not to cry out, but her leg buckled under her, and she went down hard on one knee, her racket clattering to the court. It hurt. It hurt so much it took away what breath she had left.

"Good God!"

Miles must have jumped the net, for he was at her side in an instant. She didn't look up, intent as she was on pressing the red circle on her leg, trying to hold back the pain. She was trying to hold back tears as well.

"Can you walk?"

She nodded. She couldn't talk, not just yet, not while the burning was still so keen and the tears were still so close. She'd die before she'd cry in front of him again.

Using her good leg, she pulled herself upright and took one step toward the bench. But her injured leg wouldn't accept her weight, and for a moment she feared it might fold under her again. Even knowing she couldn't walk without help, when Miles's arm came around her, she tried to push it away.

"Don't be a fool," he growled and held her tightly under her rib cage. "You can't get to the bench alone."

Gracelessly she accepted his help. Damn him, she thought miserably as she leaned into him, limping.

"Don't worry. I'm fine," she lied as they reached the bench, hoping he'd go away. It hurt worse every minute, and while he was there she had to fight away tears of anger as well as tears of pain. "Forget it."

But, as if he hadn't heard her, he straddled the bench and, ignoring her resistance, pulled her sore leg up between his legs. He folded her short white skirt back, exposing the furious, ever-reddening circle.

He drew his brows together hard and flicked a dark look at her. "I didn't mean to hurt you, you know."

"Didn't you?" The words sounded funny, coming from a throat tightened by pain. "Really?"

"No." He ran his fingers over the circle, feeling for broken skin. "I meant to beat you. I didn't mean to hurt you."

"A fine distinction," she observed flatly, willing away the goose bumps his light touch threatened to raise on her thigh. The lace of her tennis panties peeked from under her folded skirt, and she felt exposed and foolish. She tried to retrieve her leg.

"Settle down." He took her thigh in both hands and ran his thumbs hard down the long bone. He wrapped his fingers under her knee and bent it slowly up toward her chest. "Does that hurt?"

"No."

"Good. Then nothing's broken."

"Broken?" She tried to scoff. "Hardly! Your smash is good—but not that good. This is just a little bruise. You'd have to be a lot faster to break my bones."

She thought he chuckled at that, but darkness had fallen heavily and it was difficult to read his expression. The moon was hidden behind the clouds—a prologue to the tropical storm he had mentioned? she wondered briefly—and they were both just dark shadows clothed in white.

The darkness created a strange intimacy. Suddenly she was all too aware that his hands were still around her leg, his fingers nestled warmly in the hollows behind her knee. She tried again to pull free.

But again his hands held fast. As she tried to wriggle her leg free, the long muscle in his upper thigh tightened. It was a subtle, incredibly sensual movement, and her leg stilled as if paralyzed. The wet, perspiring heat of his bare thigh transferred itself to her, and she began breathing shallowly again, as if she had been running.

"Let go," she managed to say.

But he didn't. She felt his gaze on her, and was glad he couldn't see much in the darkness. She knew she was blushing.

"You're very beautiful," he said softly. "Did you know that?"

She tried to breathe, but the air was too thick with salt and jasmine, and she couldn't. "No," she said in a strangled voice. "No, Tessa is the beauty."

"Tessa is very dramatic," he agreed, his voice low, his fingers tightening. "But you have something . . . more. Something extraordinary. Quiet, but damn near irresistible."

What could she say? Her heart seemed to be traveling up her breast, toward her throat. Already a pulse pounded in hot waves under her ears.

"I should have known you would be like this," he went on, still softly. "No ordinary woman could have bewitched Evan so thoroughly. No ordinary woman could have treated him so badly and still have him coming back for more."

She yanked her leg away, wincing at the pain that shot through her thigh.

"I have not treated him badly," she cried, her anger all the more intense because of the strange tingling in her legs, a tingling that rose up toward her stomach. "Why do you keep harping on that?"

"Not harping," he said dryly, swinging his leg back over the bench. "Just observing."

He stood up. "Think you can walk now?" He patted her leg, his tone patronizing. "I've got a date in fifteen minutes and I need to clean up."

"By all means, go," she bit back, not caring that her heavy sarcasm revealed her hurt. "How foolish to waste your time with a wicked heartbreaker like me when you have an angel waiting."

He laughed out loud. "Oh, good God, not an angel, Darcy. I don't believe in angels. No, Tina's a simple, spoiled, black-haired, black-eyed beauty. And she doesn't pretend to be anything else. There's a certain refreshing honesty in that, don't you think? You should try it sometime."

And as he picked up his racket and sauntered off, Darcy found that she could forget the pain and fury long enough to register one thing. Tina was a brunette. Not a blonde.

So who was the blonde?

THE NEXT DAY she found out.

She got down to breakfast late and found Tessa and Miles chatting cozily over tea on the back porch.

"Darcy, guess what? Miles said he'd take us with him to his office today and let me watch them building a Miranda." Tessa's green eyes sparkled, as though this were a treat beyond compare.

Darcy poured herself a cup of tea from the buffet table and gave Tessa a quizzical look.

"Since when are you so interested in boats?"

Tessa laughed, unashamed. "Since last night. Brad's father is buying a Miranda, and he says it's the best boat in the world, with super jibs and mains and stuff."

Miles chuckled. "Brad comes over every day to check on her progress. Frankly, I think that's the primary attraction here."

Tessa gave Miles a stubborn pout. "So? So I think he's cute. So is that a crime?"

"Maybe a misdemeanor," Miles said, considering the issue with mock seriousness.

Tessa stuck her tongue out at him. "Can we go, Darcy?" she pleaded.

Darcy smiled at her, grateful that Miles wasn't taking his resentment out on Tessa. Tessa obviously felt quite at home here already and was well on her way to being friends with him.

Darcy couldn't think of any good reason to say no. And besides, after Miles's story about his father the other night, she was starting to be curious about the Miranda herself.

"Sure," she said. "We can go, if you'd like. Bring sunscreen."

She wasn't sure what she'd been expecting, but Hawthorne Industries, which was on mainland Fort Myers Beach, wasn't it.

It wasn't as big or as sophisticated as she had expected, judging from the income the Hawthornes clearly had. It was just a small showroom, a tiny office building and a huge yard that smelled wonderfully of wood and salt water.

Miles parked his car back in the boatyard, his BMW oddly out of place among the trucks and hot rods. But when he stepped out into the yard, in his blue corduroy shorts and his white sport shirt, he immediately had an aura of belonging. Everyone spoke to him; everyone smiled. He had an air of peace and satisfaction that Darcy hadn't seen in him before.

She looked around, curious about the place that could have such a positive, calming effect on him. Paradoxically it was almost pure chaos. Electric sanders whined, hammers pounded, sea gulls made a crazy racket overhead, and the sun was unmercifully hot. Somehow, though, the total effect was invigorating.

As she followed Miles and Tessa through the sandy area toward the office, Darcy wondered briefly why Miranda Hawthorne hadn't seen how exciting it was, with all the men, young and old alike, bare-chested, with absorbed expressions, running their hands lovingly across unvarnished hulls, doing the work they adored.

And then the blonde appeared.

She stood in the doorway of the office, staring at Darcy, a bright smile fading from her lips, as though the intense sunshine had melted it away. Darcy tried smiling at her but received only a blank, unwelcoming stare in response.

Miles finally broke away from the last of the workmen and saw the blonde himself.

"Connie!" He moved forward easily, enthusiastically. "I've brought some friends for a tour. Connie, meet Darcy and Tessa Skyler, friends of Evan's. They're waiting for him to get back from the Bahamas, and wanted to look the place over."

"Hi." The tone wasn't rude. It was just blank. She didn't meet Darcy's eyes quite squarely and turned quickly to Miles. "Are you going out with them?"

"I thought I might." He made it sound very casual. "Why, is there anything you need me for?"

Connie frowned, and Darcy got the distinct impression she was searching her mind for something, anything that would keep Miles at her side.

"Well, the dealership in Newport has put in a big order. I don't know if we can meet it. Maybe you should look the papers over."

"That can wait. Anything else?"

Reluctantly Connie shook her head. "Nothing urgent. But what about the tropical storm watch? Maybe you shouldn't . . ."

Miles shook his head. "It's still stalled in the Caribbean. We won't feel it for days yet." He gave her a quick smile. "Hey, don't worry so much."

Connie nodded reluctantly, but she didn't look happy. As the three of them turned toward the boats, Darcy thought she could feel Connie's blue eyes boring into her back. No, Connie wasn't happy at all.

An hour later, she had almost completely forgotten Connie, caught as she was in the spell of the dazzling blue water and the whispering white sails. She didn't know the first thing about mains and jibs and such, but even she could tell that the Miranda was a wonderful boat, her proud sail swollen with wind, her tall mast piercing the sky and her body skimming the water effortlessly.

Tessa, assigned to handle the jib, had scrambled onto the bow, and Darcy and Miles sat in the cockpit, in surprisingly peaceful silence, knee to knee as the gentle rock of the boat urged them together.

"Want to take her for a while?"

Darcy squinted at him, her eyelashes ruffling in the warm wind. "I don't know anything about boats," she cautioned, but the temptation was strong, and she felt her hand itching to take over.

Miles held the tiller out invitingly. "It's easy. Just hold her steady."

She couldn't resist. "I hope I don't dump us all into the Gulf," she said, laughing as she wrapped her hand around the thick pole. Immediately, as though they sensed a change of management, the sails began to droop, whacking against the mast with a terrible ruckus.

"Steady," Miles said again and put his hand over hers, guiding it gently toward the center of the boat, easing the sail away from the wind again. The clatter subsided, and the sails responded immediately to his experienced touch.

Darcy felt herself responding, too. He didn't move his hand, and his fingers pressed subtly against hers as they adjusted minutely for shifts in the wind. It was a strange intimacy, out here in the vast silence, hand over hand, slowly harnessing the power of the wind.

She didn't move her hand. To do so would have been to draw too much attention to it. He probably didn't even notice her fingers under his, probably didn't feel her heat as intensely as she was feeling his. . . .

"Does your leg still hurt?"

She looked up, surprised out of her cloying thoughts. "What?" She followed his gaze, down to where her shorts revealed the purpling bruise on her thigh. "Oh, no, not much."

"It looks terrible."

He pulled his hand away suddenly, and she protested as the tiller swayed under her grasp, threatening to loose its hold on the wind.

"No, you can do it," he said, ignoring her startled murmurings. "Just let yourself really feel it, feel which way the wind is coming from. Feel the water rushing against the rudder." He pressed her hand down hard against the tiller, and she could feel the force vibrating up through the wood and into her palm.

She glanced at him, a queer excitement tightening her muscles. "Yes," she said, struggling for detachment. "I see what you mean."

"Now." With his free hand he tilted her face toward the wind. "Feel the air against your cheek. You'll know when it changes. Feel where it's touching the sails. Feel what the sails are feeling, and give them what they want."

His words were spoken softly, with a primal sensuality that shocked her. He might have been speaking of lovemaking, not sailing. But she bowed her head and tried to do as he said.

After a few minutes, she knew what he meant. The messages from the sail were subtle, but clear if you were really listening...a little more this way, now a little more that.... It was almost as though she and the boat were one, mastering the elements, and it was an exhilarating, primitive feeling.

She smiled, looking over at Miles. "I can feel it," she said triumphantly. "It's wonderful!"

Tessa's face appeared over the cabin, pink and petulant. "Maybe we could go back now," she said, only half-politely. She had been disappointed that Brad hadn't turned up, and she wasn't hiding it very well.

"But Tessa—don't you think it's wonderful?" Now that she'd discovered this exciting affinity for sailing, Darcy could hardly bear to stop.

"Not really." Tessa clambered into the deck area with them. "You can come back another time, can't you? Evan's got one of these, too, doesn't he, Miles? When he gets home he can take you every day."

"Of course he can." Miles wrenched the tiller away from Darcy, making her hand sting as the wood burned across her grasp before she could release it. "Let's turn back. This is really a waste of time."

CHAPTER FOUR

THAT NIGHT Darcy couldn't sleep. She lay on the soft guest bed and listened to the wet lapping of the waves on the shore. She tried to think of Evan. But it was Miles's face that she saw.

That was natural, she told herself uncomfortably. Wasn't it? It had been almost a year since she had actually seen Evan, and only a few hours since she had been with Miles. And besides, Miles's personality was so dominating, his aura so forceful. It would be different when Evan returned, when she could see his smiling, gentle eyes. Then Miles's more piercing gaze would be banished from her thoughts forever.

But she had been more affected by that moment of intimacy on the boat than she liked to admit.

She kept feeling the subtle urgings of the sails on the tiller beneath her palms, and the back of her hand tingled where Miles had covered it. She had heard that sailing was relaxing—but it certainly hadn't been so for her.

Impulsively she got up and prowled toward the chest of drawers that now held her clothes. She wasn't ever going to get to sleep at this rate. She rummaged in the dark, searching for her bathing suit. Maybe a brisk swim would tire her out and help her sleep.

Finally her fingers closed around the swimsuit. It was a new one, far more daring than her old one. It had no straps, only a gold and white bandana top that tied off between her breasts, and the bottoms were fringed with a saucy skirt so tiny it was utterly frivolous.

She wondered briefly if it was prudent to wear the suit here. But, she reasoned, Miles wasn't at Two Palms tonight. Work, he had said brusquely, after they had tied the Miranda up at the dock. He hadn't even driven them back from the boat yard. He had assigned one of his employees the task of delivering them home. Her last view of him had been as he entered the small office, ready to look over the orders with Connie.

He hadn't been back to the house all day. Could he still be with Connie?

But that wasn't her business, and if she was going to swim she ought to hurry. It was really very late. And yet when she got outside she just sat, strangely disconsolate, on the edge of the pool, reluctant to go in. Tessa had gone to bed ages ago. Everything was so still that she might have been alone in the world.

The deep blue pool looked surreal, bottomless and utterly motionless under the empty, black sky. A thick cloak of clouds had smothered the stars, and the air smelled like rain, she thought, as she half-heartedly dipped her foot over the edge.

On tonight's early news the weatherman upgraded the tropical storm, and it was now officially a hurricane. Did that account for the edgy, oppressed feeling she had? Did some remnant of primal instinct warn her that danger was approaching? Did her subconscious sense that the swirling vortex of wind and rain was slowly but ineluctably headed her way?

Nonsense. She was just frustrated at having to wait so long to put her life in order. She kicked one foot, watching the white storm of bubbles rise at her heel, and wondered if it would rain before Miles came home. She hoped not. She hoped he would hurry....

Oh, for heaven's sake. Maybe she was being more unwise than she realized. Why should she care whether he got caught in the rain? He might even spend the night with Connie, who would probably be ecstatic.

Rising quickly to her feet at the tiled edge of the pool, she knifed into the water. A brisk swim would work off some of this restless energy.

The water was surprisingly cool, and it caressed her bare midriff with an intimacy she'd never felt in her old tank suit. Her nipples hardened as the water slid its wet fingers in under the flimsy kerchief top, and she swam faster, as though to outrun the strange, shivering sensuality of it all. It was almost like swimming naked—she had gone too far, she decided, when she bought this suit. Tomorrow it was back to her old one.

She did four laps without stopping, and when she finally dropped her head against the low coping at the far edge of the pool, her muscles burned and her heart was thrumming in her ears. She stretched her hands behind her, palms down on the tiles, and floated there, eyes shut, waiting for her breathing to slow. Her position lifted her breasts just clear of the water, though the heaving water lapped at the tender undersides of her arms.

Gradually the water settled to a soft undulation, and she relaxed slightly, giving herself over to sheer physical pleasure. Time telescoped, with nothing to mark it, no sound, no voices, no external signals at all. Though she did not sleep, her eyes remained shut, and her mind sank deep into the wet, silent darkness.

She didn't hear any movement, didn't feel any new currents in the water that stroked her floating body, but suddenly her eyes flew open, reacting to some unknown stimulus. And there he was, his dark eyes sparkling, his broad, sculpted chest rising from the water and an expression on his handsome features that was somehow a reflection of the tension that had been building inside her all night.

"Miles..."

The underwater lights danced frenetically as he moved toward her, his strong legs slicing the water as easily as air. Suddenly nervous, she dropped her hands and let her legs sink slowly toward the bottom. It was too deep. Her feet couldn't find the concrete, and the water closed over her face before she began to circle out with her hands.

He reached out a hand to steady her, and she smiled shakily, clinging to his fingers.

"H-hi. I was just planning to go inside," she said unconvincingly. "I think it's going to rain."

"It is," he answered, his deep voice clear and powerful in the silence. "Smell that."

As though he had willed it, she took a deep breath. He was right. The air was so thick it was like breathing water. The scent of the earth rose up, and the musty scent of grass floated over the pool. Mingled with the other smells was the dark, salty odor of the Gulf, as though the thick air had picked the scent up and carried it inland. It was definitely going to rain. There might even be a storm.

"We should go in, don't you think?" She listened for the sound of thunder, but everything was utterly silent.

"No," he said. "There's nothing to be afraid of."

"Well, of course not," she said, confused. "I just thought a storm..."

Unsure how to finish the sentence, she let go of his hand and paddled back toward the coping, like a child heading for the safety of "base" in a too-thrilling game of tag. The touch of Miles's hand had been like that, like a game that had somehow gotten out of control, a game in which the rules had mysteriously changed.

"You liked it out there today on the boat." His voice made it not a question.

She nodded, feeling somehow exposed by the admission. "Yes. Very much."

"You really felt it. Not everyone does."

She blushed. He knew, then, how sensual the experience had been. "It was—extraordinary," she admitted. "I didn't know it was so exciting."

"There's much more," he said. "Would you like me to teach you?"

She paddled away from him, disturbed by the churning in her midsection. It wouldn't be a good idea for her to spend much time with him on the Miranda. It probably wasn't even a good idea for her to spend much time with him out here. She shouldn't be feeling like this about Evan's brother....

"Maybe," she said evasively, circling again to put more distance between them. "Maybe."

She dove down, swimming hard, using a concentrated breast stroke, staying in the safe silence below the water as long as possible. When she surfaced, the length of the pool was between them, but she didn't feel any safer.

"It could be wonderful," he said, his low voice carrying clearly across the water. "With the right teacher and the right student, there's nothing in the world quite like it."

He was slowly wading toward her, and she swallowed hard. "Yes," she said, though she'd meant to say no. "Yes, please."

And then he was in front of her, and his hands were tugging her hands, skimming her body effortlessly over the water toward the long, dark column of his own. She didn't resist, even when her breasts met his chest. He eased her arms up around his shoulders and, with hands that swept silently through the sparkling water, he reached around to the small of her back, lifted and pressed her into him.

In that position, her legs, weightless, could only wrap around his waist. The muscles of her thighs, driven by instincts far below conscious thought, tightened almost imperceptibly, so that their bodies met in an intimacy that shot a white-hot arrow of pain from the point of contact up through her entire body.

But it was a pain that maddened, that made those willful muscles contract further, pushing against the heat of him, seeking the relief that lay buried in the very center of the pain.

He must have felt it, too, for his body was hard under her, and the muscles of his lean buttocks were so tight that she could feel the delineated hollows of his hips under her thighs.

"We'll start tonight, then," he whispered into her neck, as his hands found their way into her hair.

"I shouldn't—oh, God, Miles, I mustn't."

"But you will."

"No—no, I . . ."

They were stupid words, hypocritical words, and she knew it. Only the smallest part of her could hear the sound of her own voice, the sound of those impotent words. The rest of her was drowning in the flood of blood that rushed through her veins, and she could hear only the primitive beating of her heart in her ears.

And because the words were stupid, he ignored them. He let go of her back and brought his hands around between them. Mesmerized by the feel of his hard body between her legs and by the sight of those dark hands, which moved with such intoxicating slow motion under the gleaming water, she didn't protest until he'd untied the knot that held the bandana. The gold-and-white wisp of fabric floated down, down, growing fainter until it lay quiescent against the bottom of the pool.

Even then her protest was faint, almost inaudible.

"Miles. No," she said, trying to mean it. "The rain..."

He looked up, dragging his dark gaze away from her breasts, which were ethereally white, with the water boiling around them, the tiny bubbles bursting against her skin.

"No, Darcy," he said thickly. "It's already too late."

And he was right. The first drops fell even as he spoke. But they were feather-light, dusting her eyelashes, and she barely felt them. She felt instead his hands again behind the roundness of her upper thighs, lifting her, bringing her breasts up out of the cocoon of water, toward his hot mouth.

"I've wanted to do this since the first moment I saw you," he said, his lips buried in the moist hollow between her breasts. "Don't stop me."

And though she knew she should, she also knew she wouldn't. This strange, magical, drenching night was not real life. She didn't have to be afraid or ashamed or worried about tomorrow. His touch was as beautiful as she had once, long ago, back before George, dreamed a man's touch could be. And she knew, even in this moment of disorienting desire, that she might never get another chance to see a dream come true.

Her elbows dug into his broad shoulders, and her hands burrowed desperately into his hair as he licked the cool water from the rounded underside of her breasts. And then she could feel everything—a thousand things, equally, all at once, as though her senses were operating on a supernatural level. She felt his teeth as they grazed the hardened tip of her nipples; the faint tickle of her hair as it fell wetly against her back; the long, hard columns of his fingers digging into her upper thighs; even the tiny sting of raindrops against her eyelids.

Her whole body was on fire. She was a strange, burning candle that no water could extinguish. She clung to his bowed head, her fingers lost in the wet curls, as he stoked the flames in her.

The rain fell harder, as he finally released her and pushed her torso gently into the water. The water filled her ears with deafening silence, and only her face and the small, round islands of her breasts broke the surface of the water. With one bracing hand below her back to hold her afloat, he guided her through the streaming water, back toward the coping. He placed her head gently against the tiles and, one at a time, eased her arms up into the position she'd held earlier.

She opened her eyes, piercingly aware of her nakedness as her breasts lifted out of the water, their uptilted peaks puckering against the sting of the rain.

"It's all right," he murmured, sliding his hands down across her breasts, and she shut her eyes again. She had to believe him. She was wonderfully, horribly on fire, and though she had no experience to tell her so, she knew that only he could help her now.

He lifted her legs again and wrapped them lightly around his waist, raising her hips so that his hands could slowly stroke the cool, quivering flesh of her inner thighs. She moaned again, as both of his hands moved up her legs. Her breath came fast, and she clutched blindly at the tiles when his thumbs moved in to work a fiery magic. She was a spinning, flaming firework that would soon explode, turning this cool blue pool into a volcanic ocean of fire....

"You'll never marry Evan, Darcy...never."

She tried not to hear him—tried to focus on the spot within her where the flame burned brightest. But she *had* heard him, and she felt a new sensation taking over...a sinking sense of despair.

"Look at you," he insisted, his voice thick. "Look at us. Take a good look at yourself, and then tell me you'd make a fit wife for my brother."

As his words sank in, her fingers closed convulsively over the tile of the coping.

Oh, what a fool she was! Miles had been looking for a reason to hate her—a reason to keep her away from Evan—and she had made it so easy for him. She had lived right up to his expectations of her—or, rather, down to them. She shut her eyes in shame, letting the rain beat against her eyelids.

Had she believed just moments ago that she was a candle that could not be extinguished? Why hadn't she seen what a fragile flame it was? She could almost smell the acrid smoke, almost hear the hiss as the inner fire drowned, and suddenly the magical night was merely dark and cold and rainy.

She wrenched her body away from his, the separation as physically painful as if she had been tearing off a part of herself. Her feet trembled as they sought the bottom of the pool, and the ache of loss was like a knife of cold steel driven through her abdomen. It was sharp enough to bring tears to her eyes, and she was grateful for the rain that hid them.

As though in response to the change in their mood, the rain began to beat more savagely, stirring up the water until it was as opaque as the silver Gulf beyond them. Her discarded swimsuit was invisible beneath the whipped surface of the pool, but luckily the agitated water cloaked her naked body. Instinctively she bent her knees, lowering her shoulders under the wet protective covering.

Miles still hadn't reacted openly to her withdrawal. He simply stood, a dark tower rising from the boiling water around him, and watched her silently, apparently awaiting her answer.

Finally, when the pain had receded enough to allow speech and her blood had drained back down her legs, steadying her balance, she faced him with as much pride as the situation allowed.

"Because of this?" She pushed away the wet tendrils of hair that had fallen onto her face. "I fear you overestimate yourself," she said, hoping she sounded as disgusted as she felt. "I don't know why you are so determined to keep me from marrying Evan, but cheap tricks like this aren't going to work. I hardly think a few moonlight kisses are enough to make me forget the years of loyalty Evan has shown me."

His face darkened, and she saw the long muscles tense in his strong neck. "Really?" He narrowed his eyes. "Is that what this was? A few kisses? Is that the way you'll describe it to Evan?'' He spoke tightly. "Well, I hate to contradict you, but the only person I overestimated is *you*. Call me old-fashioned, but it seemed reasonable to believe that you'd draw the line at making love to your fiancé's brother.''

She flushed, a shame burning like a brand in her cheeks.

"It *was* just a few kisses! I wasn't going to—''

"Oh, yes, you were.'' He smiled, but somehow the smile didn't soften his face at all. If anything, it made his anger seem more dreadful, more hard and calculated. He whipped one hand out and cupped the small of her back, catching her off balance and drawing her to him. His rock-hard body pressed intimately against her.

"Yes, you most definitely *were*. I had wiped Evan out of your thoughts entirely.'' He pressed her closer, until she could feel every contour of his body as it buried into her softer flesh. "And I could do it again, right now, if I wanted to. . . .''

What arrogance! The fact that she was even now melting against him didn't lessen her disgust—it only increased it. She pushed her hands against his chest, ignoring the wet warmth of his skin under the whorls of dark hair, and she shoved her body free.

"You're conceited, Miles. And you're much mistaken.'' She inched backward toward the ladder, not taking her eyes from him. "Nothing on earth could make me stay here another minute. Tessa and I will be gone in the morning.''

Although she was acutely aware of her nakedness, there was now nothing to do but climb the stairs. Her towel lay across the nearest lounger, but it was several humiliating steps away, and he clearly wasn't going to offer to help her. With all the dignity she could summon, she left the swaddling waters and stalked toward the towel without looking back.

As she draped the soggy cloth around her, she heard him laugh, a bitter, mirthless sound almost smothered by the rain.

"But you'll be back, won't you, Darcy? After all, you're going to marry my brother, and we're all going to live here happily ever after. But tell me something," he added, his voice raining sarcasm. "If you can't trust yourself here with me 'another minute,' how are you going to trust yourself to be my sister-in-law for the next fifty years?"

She turned on her heel slowly, staring at him coldly through the gauze of rain that separated them.

"When Evan gets here," she said tautly, "I don't think there will be any trouble at all."

Again he laughed. "Oh, yes, I had forgotten about the power of respect and loyalty. Everyone knows that mutual respect is proof against passion any day." Still chuckling sarcastically, he moved toward the steps. "I'll have to warn Evan never to leave you alone, though. Apparently mutual respect has a rather weak transmission—it can't cover long distances."

There was no response to that. And so she turned away, the sodden towel flapping against her thighs as she ran toward the house.

SHE DIDN'T SLEEP at all. The rain that had been so benign when it pattered on the pool soon swelled into a storm. Thunder roared, arrows of lightning shot across the sky, and fists of rain pummeled her windows until she thought she would go crazy.

But the fierce storm wasn't the only thing that kept her awake. Her mind whirled with thoughts so disquieting that she couldn't have slept even in the most isolate corner of the universe.

She tried to focus on Evan's sweet smile, but as if by evil magic Miles's sardonic one superimposed itself over the image. She squeezed her eyes shut, burying her face in her knees, but nothing could make the mocking face disappear.

Why was his effect on her so powerful? No man had ever been able to reach her, affect her, the way Miles had tonight. What wretched irony that the one man who had fire in his fingertips should be the brother of the man she must marry.

But *could* she marry Evan now? She jerked out of bed and prowled toward the window, though there was nothing to see. The rain hid the moon, the Gulf, the pool, leaving nothing but oozing tracks of gray against the windowpane. It seemed to hide the answers she sought, too.

The memory of Miles's sarcastic voice vibrated around her, scoffing at her notion of "mutual respect." She squeezed the bridge of her nose hard, sighing with frustration. Until tonight she truly had believed that passion—that dizzy, drowning need other people spoke of—was not going to come to her. And because she hadn't believed herself capable of passion, it hadn't seemed a sin to marry without it.

But now she knew. Without thinking, she hugged her stomach and pressed her hot forehead against the cool glass. Now she knew so many things. Potent, dangerous things that turned the world upside down, that ripped her out of her accustomed notions and set her down, adrift, in a tumultuous sea of uncertainty. Could she marry Evan now, knowing that this capacity for passion smoldered within her? How long would it be before that passion began to burn away at her, corrupting her from the inside out?

That was what Miles had meant, what he had been trying to "teach" her out there tonight. And even if his methods were cruel, she knew that he might be right. What kind of wife could she be to Evan? He was such a decent man—didn't he deserve a wife whose passion burned for *him*—and not for his brother?

She groaned softly, her mind sore from struggling with the dilemma, and pulled the drapes shut. If only she could as easily shut out the questions that tormented her.

"Darcy? Can I come in?"

Tessa's voice startled her, and for a moment Darcy stared at her sister as though she were an alien being. Then she pulled her thoughts under control and smiled.

"Hi, honey. It's terribly late. What are you doing up?"

Tessa shuffled in, yawning, obviously still half-asleep, and plopped onto Darcy's bed. "I had a bad dream. May I stay in here?"

"Of course." Darcy arranged the covers over the younger girl and sat beside her. "Was it the storm that bothered you? It's almost over now."

Tessa bunched the pillow up under her fist and snuggled her cheek comfortably against it. "No, I like the rain," she murmured. "It was George."

Darcy's heart skipped a beat. "What do you mean?"

"George. I had a nightmare about George." Tessa opened her eyes suddenly, and their green depths were troubled. "He's going to be mad, isn't he, Darcy? Because we left."

Darcy tried to smile reassuringly. "Probably," she admitted. "But he'll get over it."

Tessa's eyes fluttered shut. "Yeah. I guess so. But you know what?"

"What, honey?"

Tessa smiled, her eyes still closed. "It's nice here."

Darcy's throat closed miserably. "Yes, it is," she murmured, reaching out to pat her sister's soft cheek. "It sure is...."

But Tessa was already asleep. She looked so vulnerable. And so naive. That was partly Darcy's fault. She had babied her little sister shamelessly. And yet she knew she would do it again. Better to be young and innocent too long than never to be young at all.

But what was she to do now? Marriage had seemed the only answer. Just running away wouldn't do. Even if she had been willing to leave Skyler Stores behind, if she had been willing to run away and get a job of her own somewhere, that wouldn't have helped her to protect Tessa. George had legal custody of Tessa and would never have let Darcy take her away. And now that he had so clearly awakened to her loveliness—

No, marriage was the only hope. When she married, she gained control of Skyler Stores, and with that power she could force George to give her custody of Tessa.

And she couldn't marry just anyone. Mr. Stone, her father's lawyer, had to approve the marriage, as a safeguard against "fortune hunters." Evan Hawthorne, who was quite wealthy in his own right, would pass that test with flying colors. And no one could look at Evan's gentle face and doubt his sincerity.

But could she marry him? Could she lock these new, disturbing feelings away? Perhaps she could. She was strong. For most of her life, she'd had to rely on her own good sense and her own inner strength. For Tessa's sake, perhaps she could do it again.

But as she sat on the edge of the bed, her hand wrapped protectively around her sister's foot, watching the black sky lighten to gray, to silver and finally to the pink-edged pearl of dawn, she could still feel the touch of Miles's lips against her skin. . . .

THE ONLY CERTAINTY the dawn brought was that she and Tessa must leave Two Palms. She didn't trust Miles—and she wasn't sure she trusted herself just yet. She needed time to build her resolve, to harden her heart and her body against him. And then when Evan came home . . .

But she'd take it one step at a time. First she had to get through the morning—and find the courage to face Miles after the fiasco of last night. Sighing, she pulled on an old pair of knee-length blue jeans and an aqua T-shirt and was running a brush through her hair when someone knocked at her door.

"It's open, Alice," she called from the dressing room. Was it nine o'clock already? She must have been daydreaming. But the maids at Two Palms were certainly efficient. You could set your watch by their schedules. She grabbed a barrette and clipped her hair back from her face.

"I believe this is yours."

Her hands froze at the back of her head, and her eyes flew to the reflection behind her in the mirror. Not the maid. Miles. One side of his mouth turned up as he watched her obvious dismay.

"I'm sorry. I thought you were Alice." She let her hands fall slowly and tried to arrange her face. She didn't feel ready for this encounter. But perhaps she wouldn't *ever* feel ready. "She usually cleans my room each morning."

"I know." She heard the note of amusement. Of course. He had probably set up the housekeeping schedule himself. The one-sided smile deepened nastily. "I could have asked her to bring this up to you, I suppose. But somehow I thought you'd prefer me to deliver it privately."

Finally she noticed what he held in his hands, and a hot flush inched its way across her face and neck. Her bathing suit top. In his strong fingers, its wisp of gold-and-white fabric looked as tiny as doll clothes. Her stomach knotted, and she had to force her hand out to accept it.

"Thank you," she said stiffly, dropping it onto the vanity counter as though it burned her fingers. When had he retrieved it? Had anyone else seen it?

"I brought it in last night." One brow was quirked now, marking his amusement at the anxieties that marched across her face so blatantly.

"Thank you," she said again, a hint of dismissal in her voice. Why didn't he leave? He was standing too close. From where she sat his long, tanned legs were just at eye level. He must have been playing tennis. He was dressed in his white shorts and shirt, and he smelled faintly damp, sun-baked and disturbingly masculine. Confused by her body's intense reaction to him she fumbled in the vanity drawer, looking for a lipstick, a blusher, earrings, anything that would distract her.

But, either oblivious to or amused by her discomfort, he leaned against the wall, his hands in the pockets of his tennis shorts, and watched her. Under his silent scrutiny, her hands shook. Finally her fingers closed around the cool silver tube of a lipstick, and she drew it out and began applying the color with exaggerated care.

"I'd better get going," she said awkwardly as the pink tip of the lipstick slid across her lower lip. "Alice will want to clean in here."

"Alice can wait."

She glanced at him, surprised by the firm tone, and then went back to stroking her lips. "But there's no need. I'm almost finished."

"Yes, there is. I want to talk to you."

Slowly she twisted the pink stick down into its container and, dropping it back into the drawer with a clatter, swiveled on the vanity stool to face him. She squared her shoulders instinctively. "About what?"

"About last night, of course." His brows contracted, as though he were irritated by her question. "Don't you think we should?"

But she was irritated, too. "No, I don't. Not now or ever. Last night was a terrible mistake. I'm sorry it happened, but it's too late to undo it now. The best I can do is promise you it won't ever happen again."

His brows lowered even further, shadowing his eyes. "Can you really promise that?" he asked, unsmiling.

She nodded, forcing herself to meet his dark eyes steadily. "Yes. I think we should just try to forget it ever happened."

A muscle in his jaw leaped, and though she winced at his obvious displeasure, she continued. "I'll explain it to Evan, if you insist that he be told. But I honestly believe it would serve no purpose. It could only hurt him."

"Too bad you didn't think of that last night," he said, his voice rough.

"Or you," she returned, refusing to be cowed. "It took two of us to make that particular mistake."

He looked so very angry, with his eyes as black as coals and his lips pressed hard and white together, that she wondered if she had gone too far. Her courage fading, she looked back toward the mirror, where her pale face and hollowed eyes spoke of her anguished night of indecision.

"So you still think you can pull this off?" His voice was raspy, as though his anger had scraped it raw. "Even after last night, you still think you deserve to marry Evan? You still think I'll *let* you?"

He moved behind her, and his white-clad body dominated the mirror, but she fastened her eyes on her own reflection. Staring fixedly into the shadowed, tormented eyes that looked back at her, she merely nodded her answer.

"Well, I won't." Rage tightened his words, and in her peripheral vision she saw one fist clench at his side. "I won't let you ruin his life."

She rose in a flash of fury, nearly toppling the fragile vanity chair in her haste. "Just who do you think you are?" she demanded, wheeling to confront him. "You can't stop me. Evan *cares* about me, don't you understand that? And I care about him. You can't turn him against me, no matter what you tell him."

His hand closed over her shoulder. "You're a liar. You don't give a damn about him. You never have. You proved that last night. You're an opportunist, but you've lost your opportunity to fool Evan. I'll disillusion him about you in a hurry if you don't leave him alone."

Anger, anxiety, guilt and fear churned her emotions until she felt them swelling, burning in her chest. She had been through too much. She was tired of fighting—fighting George, fighting Miles, fighting her own rebellious passions. She only wanted somewhere safe to rest.

"Stop it," she said, struggling to get the words past the lump that clogged her throat. She spoke more vehemently because of her own uncertainty. "Stop it!" She put her hands up to catch the tears that threatened to spill across her hot cheeks.

For a crazy moment she considered telling him the whole truth, about George and Tessa and the whole sickening mess. But his angry fingers were hurting her, and his face was tense and grim. He would never understand.

"Do whatever you want," she cried, trying to pull away from his punishing fingers. "Just get out of here and leave me alone."

She didn't hear the low knock. She knew only that Miles's hand tightened further on her shoulder, and he turned toward the door.

"Yes?" His voice was only partly under control, and when Darcy turned, too, she saw a bewildered look on Alice's pretty features.

"I'm sorry," Alice began uncertainly, looking from Miles to Darcy. The room must have smelled of emotion, and Darcy swallowed hard, still trying to force down the lump there.

"That's all right," Miles interrupted. "What is it?"

"It's Mr. Evan," Alice explained hastily, obviously eager to escape. "His car just drove in. You told me to tell you as soon as he—"

Evan! Darcy tried to move toward the door, propelled by her desperate need to escape Miles's angry face. Evan was here. Evan, whose gentle face never looked like that, whose fingers would never have gripped her shoulder so tightly.

"Darcy, wait." Miles's hand was still on her, holding her in the room.

"No," she said, pulling against the pressure, not looking back. "I have to see him."

"Let me go first."

She turned and glared into his dark eyes. "No," she said, the sound sharp enough to stab the air between them. "I want to see him myself. I want to *tell* him myself, if he must be told. Let me go."

For a minute she thought he wouldn't. His mouth was a grim line, and his hand held her so tightly she could feel the grind of bone on bone. But finally his grip eased, and his hand dropped.

"Perhaps you should be first, at that," he said, falling back with elaborate courtesy. "But Evan may have a little surprise for you, too. After you, Miss Skyler."

CHAPTER FIVE

HER FEET didn't seem to touch a single one of the stairs as she flew down them. She had to get to Evan quickly—quickly, before Miles did.

Her heart hammered in her throat as she entered the big, sun-drenched greatroom and saw him standing by the window. She stopped, the adrenaline bleeding out of her as if from a wound. Evan....

But the sight of him was enough to clear her muddied mind. She knew the truth in an instant—she could never marry him. He was not a theoretical savior, a cinema-hero knight in shining armor. He was just Evan—a real person, a good friend, a fine man, but a man she didn't love and never would.

The truth was bitter, for it meant there never had been any sanctuary, not really. Oh, God, she had failed Tessa completely. All that running, all that hoping—and all wasted. She could never have married Evan, not even if Miles had never kissed her. And now that he had...

She couldn't say anything. She couldn't bring herself to go to Evan, not even when she heard Miles approach from behind her and stand quietly, waiting to witness the reunion.

Evan turned away from the window, blinking as his eyes adjusted to the change in light. He frowned gently and seemed to be trying to get his bearings.

"Well, Darcy?" Miles muttered. "Don't you have something to say to Evan?"

"Darcy?" Evan spoke the word as though bewildered. "Is that you, Darcy?"

"Yes," she answered and waited for the eager leap of happiness that always brightened his eyes at the sight of her. "Yes, Evan. It's Darcy."

But surprisingly, his eyes clouded over, and his gentle frown grew deeper and more distressed than she had ever seen it. A guilty spasm shot through her. Oh, no. Did he know already? Had someone seen her in the pool last night—drenched and abandoned in Miles's arms—and told Evan already? Her mouth went dry, and she seemed to know no words, no language at all. She'd said that last night didn't matter, but suddenly it seemed shameful if it could cause Evan this much unhappiness. Even if she didn't want to marry him, she didn't want to hurt him.

"I can't believe you're here, Darcy." Evan seemed to be struggling to find words, too. "It's such a surprise. I haven't heard from you in so long…and I, well, I was meaning to write…or call…."

And then there were other movements—a rustling in the shadows of the doorway. Darcy and Evan both looked toward the sound as though mesmerized.

The movements took a shape. Young. Very young—no more than eighteen. Diminutive. Black-haired. Blue-eyed. Lovely. Shy. Darcy stared, as confused as if the shape weren't human.

"Hi," the shape said in a voice so sweet and self-effacing and with a smile so gentle it tugged at Darcy's heart in spite of her turmoil. "I'm Emily."

The sweet sounds exerted a power over Evan, too. He leaped to the girl's side and wrapped his slim arm around her tiny shoulders. Even through her befuddlement Darcy saw that there, around *those* shoulders, Evan's arms acquired a new strength.

"Oh, Emily, I'm sorry." Suddenly his tenderness was far from ineffectual. It was a profoundly moving show of protection. Darcy squinted, as though seeing Evan for the first time. "Emily, this is a very good friend of mine, Darcy Skyler. Darcy, this is Emily. We're—" he looked at Emily with undisguised pride "—we're going to get married. We rushed home to make the announcement."

He looked at Darcy, then, and his soft brown eyes asked for understanding. He had waited, the eyes seemed to say, for so long, without hope. And then Emily had come to him. . . .

And in spite of everything, Darcy *did* understand. This was what Evan had always wanted—what he'd always deserved. This, not Darcy, was the love of Evan's life. Emily of the soft eyes was the woman who could make him a man.

And she was glad, so glad for him. Her plans had been dust long before she set eyes on Emily. Miles was right. She would have been a terrible wife to Evan.

She managed a smile. "How wonderful, Evan," she said. "It's just wonderful." But still she couldn't move. With every passing second her own predicament was becoming clearer, and she wondered if her shock-weakened legs would hold her much longer.

Evan looked grateful for her words, but his eyes still held a question. "What are you—" He stopped and tried again. "What brings you to Sanibel, Darcy? I mean, is there anything. . ." He stumbled again, apparently lost between his desire to assist her and his helpless inability to keep his earlier promises.

She shook her head, trying to think of comforting words and wondering if she could say them without crying, even if she *could* think of them. She was happy for him, she really was. But what was she going to do? What on earth was she going to *do*?

"She came to see me."

Miles's deep voice sounded from almost at her ear, and his hands slid up to caress her shoulders. At first his words bewildered her—she had come to see *him?*—but as the hard warmth of his hands worked up to her neck, she understood what he was doing. He was protecting Evan, and having a wonderful time, humiliating her. He had known about Emily—had known all along. Her muscles stiffened with her suppressed rage. What a cruel little game he had been playing! He could have telephoned Evan whenever he wanted to, she thought suddenly. He'd been deliberately stalling, hoping to give Evan and Emily enough time to settle on an engagement, or perhaps just hoping to force her into giving up before Evan came back.

Fury made speech impossible.

"You?" Evan clearly was still confused, and his face reflected it. "I didn't know you'd ever even met Darcy, Miles."

"I hadn't," Miles answered smoothly, his voice deep and affectionate, "until...a couple of weeks ago. I met her in Georgetown, and I persuaded her to bring Tessa down for a visit."

He dipped his head and dropped a kiss on Darcy's ear. The touch sent shivers through her. She wanted to wheel around and slap him. Damn his arrogance, his cruelty! Probably he'd had been looking forward to her downfall today with relish. What a hateful man he was.

Evan looked alight with relief. "Well!" he exclaimed. "Well, how about that? That's great!"

Emily smiled, too.

The next few minutes passed in a blur. Everything was polite, Darcy was sure of that, and everyone was shaking hands and smiling and filling the room with a familial bliss. But she might as well have been a mannequin, posing in all the right attitudes, a plastic smile affixed to her lips, while a hurricane of emotions churned within her.

When, finally, an excuse presented itself, she left them. She ascended the stairs, so softly that her feet didn't make a sound on the carpet, and she entered her pretty room, closing the door quietly behind her. And then she sank onto the edge of the bed. She wondered, in a detached way, why she didn't cry. Certainly her prospects were as dire as they ever had been.

And yet she didn't. She didn't feel sad. She felt only fury. Miles Hawthorne had played her for a fool, all right. He'd manipulated her into the most humiliating position possible. No, she couldn't feel sorrow now. She was consumed with hatred.

She just sat, staring at her hands, so newly tanned, folded neatly in her lap, until a light rap sounded at the door.

"Come in," she called stiffly. She knew who it was. She had wondered how long it would be before Miles came up to gloat.

"Are you okay?"

It was Miles. She squeezed her hands tightly. "Yes. I'm fine. That must disappoint you."

Without hesitation Miles firmly closed the door and came into the room. He settled himself on a comfortable armchair next to the window and watched her for a moment.

"It might if I believed you were. But I don't—I think you're quite wretched, actually."

She looked up at his appraising gaze and instinctively folded her arms across her chest, as though to protect her heart's secrets. "And that pleases you."

He raised his brows. "Surprisingly, not as much as I thought it would." One corner of his mouth twisted up. "But you had it coming, you know. He'd been through hell for you."

"You knew all along, didn't you? About Emily?"

He nodded. "She went with him on the delivery. I didn't know he'd ask her to marry him this trip. I didn't mention it because I wanted them to have some time together before he came back and saw you here."

She stood up, her eyes narrowed. "No—you didn't mention it because you wanted to embarrass me. You got a kick out of that scene down there, you arrogant—"

"Now, now, don't lose your temper." He stood, too. "I told you, I didn't know they were getting engaged yet. I wouldn't have set you up for that. I wouldn't have needed to. If I'd known Evan was that serious, I wouldn't have worried so much about him seeing you."

She turned away with a tsk of disgust.

"Oh, come on, Darcy. Truce. Let's be practical. You've got a problem—unless you've already set a new course."

"A what?"

"A new course. In case Evan didn't come through for you. You've been sailing a bit close to the wind, you know. You're going to have to come about, aren't you, and try another tack."

She wanted to slap him. But she kept her arms crossed tightly and, turning, contented herself with offering him a withering glare. "Would you please stop talking in sailing metaphors and just tell me what you mean? I never got those sailing lessons, remember? Thank God. What are you talking about?"

"I'm talking about the fact that you, Darcy Skyler, have got to get married." One dark brow went up in derisive amusement. "I've known all along it wasn't Evan you wanted—just a wedding ring. Husband Anyone will do. As long as you can become Mrs. Anyone, you're free, free to take over Skyler Stores. I'm right, aren't I? It's driving you crazy to have George in control of the stock, and you were willing to use my brother to get your hands on it."

She couldn't help it. She was gaping. How did he know all that? "How—" she began, outrage strangling her words.

"Tessa," he filled in cooperatively, smiling wickedly, "is a bit naive for her age, don't you think? She'd tell anybody anything. We'll definitely have to warn her not to tell Evan the truth about your impromptu vacation here in Sanibel."

"You've been pumping a fifteen-year-old for information?" Her disgust made her reckless. "How charming!" She rose from the bed—she didn't want to sit that close to him. She didn't want to sit at all—every muscle in her screamed out for action. What had she been waiting for? She should have been packing all along. Her heart galloping with the mindless, uncontrollable anger of a hurt beast, she yanked her suitcase out of the closet and tossed it violently onto the bed.

"What are you doing?" He stood up, too.

She threw fistfuls of clothing into the open case, not caring what happened to the fabrics. "It should be obvious. I'm leaving."

"Hey, there. Settle down." He stayed her arm by wrapping his long fingers around her wrist. "Where are you going to go? Home to George?" He let the thought sink in before continuing. "No, I don't think so. Well, I have a better idea."

She didn't look at him. She couldn't. Her cheeks were burning, and her breath was coming hard. She couldn't bear to see the amused smirk on his lips.

"Don't you want to hear it? I think you'll like it." He pulled on her arm, turning her slightly toward him. Like a recalcitrant child, she kept her eyes on the floor.

With a small, self-satisfied chuckle—he seemed to find her discomfiture appropriate—he put his fingers under her chin and lifted her face toward his. "If you can't stand to look at me, this is going to be a bit more difficult. Generally, proposals of marriage are made between people who *enjoy* looking at each other."

Her eyes widened, and her lips fell open. Her deep breathing stopped altogether, and she grew light-headed. Had she misheard him? She must have.

"Well, what do you think?" He squeezed her chin between his fingers, as if to demand her attention. "It's really rather neat, isn't it? You just need to be Mrs. Anybody, so why not be Mrs. Miles Hawthorne?"

The ivory silk underclothes she had been holding slithered out of her grasp, puddling on the green bedspread like spilled milk. She stared, disbelieving, at his unsmiling face.

Mrs. Miles Hawthorne... Somehow, even though his phrasing sounded lighthearted and even though the idea was insane, she knew he wasn't kidding. His dark brown eyes squared with hers, and they held no mischievous lights, no sadistic pleasure over a secret jest. They were speculative perhaps, as if he were trying to anticipate her answer.

She *couldn't* take such a suggestion seriously. "You must be joking," she said weakly, in spite of her conviction that he wasn't.

"Why?"

She frowned, unsure how to answer him. "It's preposterous," she said finally, looking down to where his hand held her wrist. The fact that he had to restrain her physically somehow seemed to make it even more preposterous.

"Why?" His monotone suggested an infinite patience with the subject, a patience that his tightened grip contradicted. "Be more specific."

"I can't," she said, shaking her head helplessly. "It's—it's everything. We hardly know each other, but what we do know we intensely dislike. Any thought of love—"

"Love?" For the first time he seemed angry, and his lips tightened. "What does that have to do with it? You were perfectly willing to marry Evan without *love*."

"But I care about him—"

"Oh, for God's sake, don't let's go into *that* again," he broke in, frustration edging his voice. "It doesn't matter, anyway. We have something better than love, better even than your famous mutual respect."

"What?"

The minute she asked she was sorry. While still holding her wrist captive with one hand, he used the other to caress her bare arm, trailing his fingers from the elbow up to the curve of her shoulder. She couldn't stop the shivers from speckling her arm or from spreading across her chest. Suddenly her clothes seemed too tight, pressing against her skin.

Last night. They had last night. And if she agreed to this crazy scheme, there would be more nights, more drenching, fiery nights....

He laughed, a low, triumphant sound, as his fingers ran back down her arm, tracing the path of shivers. "Ummm. Well, yes, we have that. But, actually, that wasn't what I meant."

She flushed and tried to pull her arm away.

Still smiling unpleasantly, he finally let go. His sudden acquiescence surprised her, and she stumbled back. "We have the most time-honored reason of all for forging an alliance," he said. "We have a common enemy."

She tilted her head, stunned, forgetting her embarrassment for the moment. "Who?"

"George, of course." His smile was most disagreeable as he dropped himself back onto the armchair. "I probably don't hate him as much as you do, but I run a close second."

"George?" She sank onto the bed, next to the crumpled mound of clothes and tried to make sense of it all. "Why do *you* hate George? I thought he was just an old college acquaintance of yours. You acted as though you knew him only slightly—hardly well enough to hate him."

"Some might say that to know George *is* to hate him," he responded, hooking one arm over the back of the chair. His tone was light, but something hard and brittle lay under it. "Actually, though, in my case the reason's more specific. I told you that George and I have known each other a long time—since our college days. Well, we've clashed more times than I can count, over more things than I could remember, through the years. I suppose our temperaments just don't mix well— we're both men who know what we want, and occasionally we've wanted the same thing.''

His eyes were dark, and she thought she glimpsed the hatred he professed buried somewhere in their depths. She shivered again at the sight. Miles Hawthorne might not be anything like George in most ways—but he certainly was an enemy as formidable.

''Anyhow,'' he went on, recovering his light tone, ''George has decided he wants stock in Hawthorne Industries. He's been buying every share he can get his hands on.''

Her eyes widened. Suddenly his hatred made more sense to her. She could relate to this dilemma, having spent the past six years watching George interfere in *her* company, too. And she had sensed, from Miles's conversations, that Hawthorne Industries was terribly important to him. It had been the only steady thing in a pretty rocky life.

''Oh, I see,'' she said. ''How awful! How many outstanding shares are there? Can he get control?''

He shook his head. ''No, I don't think so. Evan and I own a big block between us, and many of our biggest holders are quite loyal to us. But he can be a damned thorn in my side, which is all he really wants, anyhow. And, of course, he wants a profit. He's already indicated he'd be willing to sell back the stock—at an absurdly inflated price.''

She nodded thoughtfully. Wasn't that just like George? He derived a twisted pleasure from making other people miserable. ''But what does this have to do with—'' she didn't know how to put it ''—with my marrying you?'' One miserable interpretation occurred to her right away. "Does it merely strike you as funny? A sick poetic justice—a sort of you-take-mine-and-I'll-take-yours revenge?" Her anger was rising again, replacing the momentary sympathy she'd felt. "I don't believe I'd enjoy being the pawn in your nasty little chess game."

"For God's sake, come down off your high horse!" He looked impatient, his eyes narrow and his lips tight. "Do you think I'd bother with such nonsense? I'm talking about a straightforward business deal. I'll put the Mrs. in front of your name, which brings Skyler Stores under your control. In return, you'll agree to have Skyler Stores sell us back our stocks at the fair market price."

"But if George bought those stocks—"

"George?" He made the word sound like a curse. "Where would George get that kind of money on his own? Use your head. He's been using Skyler Stores' assets to buy my stock. *He* doesn't own it. Right now Skyler Stores does. But George would likely find a way to finagle them into his own name, given time."

"Oh." Of course. Humbled, she knew she deserved his sarcasm. Naturally George couldn't have afforded such a thing. Before he married her mother, George had been in charge of public relations at the country club—which essentially meant he'd been in charge of flattering middle-aged ladies who hung around the pool while their husbands golfed. Occasional fringe benefits did accrue from particularly gullible ladies but nothing substantial enough to let him freewheel on Wall Street.

"So you see what a sensible proposition it is." He leaned back, his attitude smug, as though he knew he couldn't fail. "It will work."

The total self-assurance stung her. She hated the way he took her acquiescence for granted. And wasn't it all just a bit hypocritical?

"What strikes me first," she said slowly, trying to hang on to her temper, "is how ironic it is for you, who so despised me for being willing to marry Evan to solve my problems, to be suggesting the same thing for yourself."

At first she thought she had scored a direct hit. His brown eyes flashed, and his arms clenched, as though he were going to rise abruptly. But he covered the minute display smoothly and remained seated.

"That was different," he explained, as he might to a child. "Evan fancied himself in love with you. I simply thought it was selfish of you to take advantage of his infatuation to achieve your own ends." He hitched one long leg over the other and smiled, but it didn't blunt the sharp edge of his words. "On the other hand, with the bargain I've proposed, no one is taking advantage of anyone. We both know where we stand. We both give a little—we both get a lot."

She flushed, knowing full well exactly what the subtext of his message was. You can't hurt me, he was saying, because, unlike Evan, I don't care two figs for you. Well, that couldn't come as a surprise. Ever since she had arrived he'd treated her with contempt, up to and including the interlude in the pool last night. Perhaps, she realized with a sharp pang across her chest, that had been the most contemptuous moment of all. He had been willing to humiliate her just to prove his point, willing to manipulate her body and her desires just to prove her unworthy of Evan. And all the while he'd known Evan wouldn't marry her. All the while he'd known about Emily. The rest had been just for the pleasure of hurting her.

A completely irrational sense of misery swept over her, and she had to struggle to keep from crying or lashing out or running away, or doing something crazy. Crazy because she already knew she should accept his offer. It was, in its way, a godsend.

And why, after all, should this proposition fill her with such unhappiness? She *had* been willing to marry Evan without loving him. Why should the prospect of *this* particular loveless marriage seem so empty, so potentially heartbreaking?

He was being honest. She should appreciate that. And yet, how different it might have been if he'd just embraced her again, if he'd told her that last night had started something special....

"Well? Why do you look as if I've just broken your heart? I think it's a pretty fair offer." His gaze, suddenly penetrating and searching, swept her face. "Or is it Evan who broke it? Is it possible that I misjudged your feelings for him? Does Emily's presence hurt more than your pride?"

She looked up miserably. His bitter tone was like a whip against already sore wounds. "No," she said slowly. "No, I'm happy for Evan. She's good for him—I can tell it already."

"Yes, she is," he agreed tartly. "Much better than you ever were. She worships him."

"But what about you? What about love?" She thought suddenly of Connie. "Don't you want to marry for love?"

"Not really." He moved closer, out of the shadows and toward the bed, where she stood, rigid with a frantic sense of doom. His dark brows were low over his hard eyes as he went on. "Remember, I don't believe in angels. Actually, we make a pretty good match. You watched your mother make a fool of herself with all those husbands. Well, I watched my father die of a broken heart for a woman who wasn't worth it, a woman who didn't give a damn about him."

He took hold of her shoulders firmly, as if to transmit his conviction to her through touch. "So, you see, we're made for each other. Two cynics whose only real passion is business." He raised his brows. "Just be practical, Darcy. George mustn't be allowed to run Skyler Stores anymore, and he mustn't be allowed to buy any more of Hawthorne Industries. Our marriage will accomplish that. Is it a bargain, then?"

She nodded. A bargain. Her eyes felt sandy. All the tears she might have cried were buried beneath the sand.

"You know we'll have to make it look real," she said slowly. "The will stipulates that my father's lawyer, Mr. Stone, must approve the marriage. He was worried about . . . fortune hunters."

He laughed. "Good God! Well, I've no need of any of your pretty bank accounts. I think a quick check of my assets will put those fears to rest."

She knew it was true—she had already considered that detail when she'd hoped to marry Evan. His laughter, his insouciance in the face of her distress irritated her.

"What about—what was her name? Tina? If we're going to convince Mr. Stone, you'll have to forgo the pleasures of frankly spoiled beauties for quite a while."

"Of course." He still looked amused. "Tina will survive—thrive, even. Thriving is her specialty."

She shook her head at his tone. "Isn't there *anyone* you care about? Isn't there anyone you can't give up to please Mr. Stone?"

Finally his grin dropped. He looked at her through squinted eyes. "Well, there is someone," he said, his voice casual. "You met her at the boat yard. But I think your Mr. Stone will understand about Connie. After all, she is an employee, and she's been a family friend since we were all children."

One corner of his mouth curled up. "Surely even an affianced gentleman is allowed to have a couple of left-over childhood friends," he said. "And besides, you're a good enough actress, aren't you, to persuade everyone that we've fallen madly, suddenly, in love?"

She stared at him, weary, confused. "I guess so."

"Good." He looked grimly satisfied. "Cheer up, Darcy. It's only for three years." He put his hand under her chin again, tilting her lips toward his. "And who knows? We might get to those sailing lessons after all. I have a feeling that together we could really run the wind."

Her lips began to tingle, the only part of her body that felt anything at all. No. No. No....

"No," she heard herself saying out loud. "No! Not that..."

He dropped his hand abruptly. "No?" His eyes clouded over again, and he watched her from behind their unfathomable blankness. "Fine. Perhaps you're right. It might be cleaner without that."

He moved toward the door. "Better unpack before Tessa gets home," he said over his shoulder, glancing at the heap on the bed. "We're going to have enough explaining to do as it is."

CHAPTER SIX

THE SMALL island church was really quite beautiful in its quiet way. No stained glass or gilded altars awed the spirit, but a wonderful simplicity of honey pine, white walls and arched windows soothed the soul.

Or would have, if the soul in question hadn't been quite so agitated.

Darcy's heart was beating so fast she had to breathe through her mouth to get enough air. And then her mouth was too dry, and she had to lick her lips so that they wouldn't stick to her teeth. So much for the clichéd blushing bride. This bride was as pale as a ghost.

She couldn't even hear the minister. When she wasn't trying to keep from fainting, she was listening to Miles's breathing, which was annoyingly even and slow. He hadn't shifted his position even once since the ceremony had started—his body was completely calm and at ease. Damn the superb confidence of the man. You might have thought he got married every day.

In embarrassing contrast, she was practically vibrating. Her white dress, which reminded her of the one she'd worn to Great-Aunt Susan's garden party when she was only eight, was quivering in the sunlight, as though her racing blood shook it. And the taffeta petticoat she wore under it betrayed her restlessness with its infernal rustling.

You may be the winner of the

MILLION DOLLAR GRAND PRIZE!

TO BE
ELIGIBLE,
AFFIX THIS
STICKER TO
SWEEPSTAKES
ENTRY FORM

FOR A
CHANCE AT
THOUSANDS
OF OTHER
PRIZES, ALSO
AFFIX THIS
STICKER TO
ENTRY FORM

TO GET FREE
BOOKS AND
GIFTS, AFFIX
THIS STICKER
AS WELL!

ENTER HARLEQUIN'S *BIGGEST* SWEEPSTAKES EVER!

IT'S FUN! IT'S FREE!
AND YOU COULD BE A
MILLIONAIRE!

Your unique Sweepstakes Entry Number appears on the Sweepstakes Entry Form. When you affix your Sweepstakes Entry Sticker to your Form, you're in the running, and you could be the $1,000,000.00 annuity Grand Prize Winner! That's $33,333.33 every year for up to 30 years!

AFFIX BONUS PRIZE STICKER

to your Sweepstakes Entry Form. If you have a winning number, you could collect any of 8,617 prizes. And we'll also enter you in a special bonus prize drawing for a new Ford Mustang and the "Aloha Hawaii Vacation"!

AFFIX FREE BOOKS
AND GIFTS STICKER

to take advantage of our Free Books/Free Gifts introduction to the Harlequin Reader Service®. You'll get four brand-new Harlequin Presents® novels, plus a lovely Victorian Picture Frame and a mystery gift, absolutely free!

NO PURCHASE NECESSARY!

Accepting free books and gifts places you under no obligation to buy a thing! After receiving your free books, if you don't wish to receive any further volumes, write "cancel" on the shipping document and return it to us. But if you choose to remain a member of the Harlequin Reader Service®, you'll receive six more Harlequin Presents® novels every month for just $2.24* each—51¢ below the cover price, with no additional charge for delivery! You can cancel at any time by dropping us a line, or by returning a shipment to us at our cost. Even if you cancel, your first four books, your lovely Victorian Picture Frame and your mystery gift are absolutely free—our way of thanking you for giving the Reader Service a try!

*Terms and prices subject to change without notice.
Sales tax applicable in NY. © 1991 HARLEQUIN ENTERPRISES LIMITED.

The dress had been Tessa's idea. Darcy had wanted a simple linen suit, but Tessa'd refused. The whole idea of the wedding delighted her. Her romantic heart had never much liked the idea of the marriage to Evan, and now she thought a love-at-first-sight story was just *too* perfect.

So in her usual ebullient way, Tessa had hauled Darcy along for the ride, scouring the stores on both Sanibel and nearby Fort Myers for the perfect wedding dress, the perfect bouquet, the perfect wedding cake. Once or twice during the period Darcy had caught Miles's amused gaze and had had to turn away, flushing. Clearly he thought they were two little girls playing dress up. And since both he and Darcy knew that there was nothing of the fairy tale in this wedding, he must have found their planning ridiculous.

But it wasn't ridiculous. It was, in some way she couldn't explain, both frightening and exhilarating. She tried to listen to the minister.

"I will."

The two small words drove a sharp, fine nail into Darcy's heart. Spoken in Miles's deep baritone, they sounded so solemn, so true. And yet she knew they were only a masquerade. This marriage was a business arrangement, not a sacrament.

And now it was her turn. She found her voice, though it trembled slightly, and the fear that she might faint grew stronger.

"I will," she whispered, the wooden floor seeming to tilt under her feet. She couldn't meet the minister's eyes. It seemed a sacrilege to make the promise of "till death" when she knew herself to be taking out only a limited three-year contract—and yet no bolt of lightning struck her down. Did God forgive liars, then, if their motives were pure?

When Miles took her hand, he must have felt the tremor, for he steadied it quickly with a firm squeeze. He met her eyes briefly, squinting as if surprised. Then he bent to put the ring on her finger.

It was the most beautiful ring she'd ever seen—an antique, wide circlet of intricately wrought golden flowers, each studded with a gem, alternating rubies and diamonds. She had protested when he showed it to her. It was too beautiful, too special. A three-year, business-deal marriage could be marked with a simple band. Save the rubies and diamonds for a real wedding....

And yet he had insisted. Every eldest Hawthorne son for a hundred years had put it on his bride's finger, and he refused to break with tradition. She could simply give it back after the marriage ended, he had suggested curtly. There was a Hawthorne tradition of that, too. And confused and embarrassed by his bitter references to his mother, she had given in rather than argue.

Now the ring slipped onto her slender finger easily. She'd lost a few pounds in the past week from being up all night wrestling with her emotions and running all day shopping for bridal gee-gaws. It slid toward her knuckle, and instinctively she curled her fingers, catching it. Its cold filigree dug into her shaking fingertips, but its solid weight was somehow reassuring. Oddly she felt in that instant that she was no longer an orphan. Now she was a wife. She didn't have to fight George alone. Miles was her husband, and he would stand beside her.

Gratitude emboldened her, and she found the courage to smile up at his solemn face. He didn't smile back.

His eyes were locked darkly on her lips, and she felt them tremble under his gaze. The smile faded away....

"You may kiss the bride."

As Miles bent toward her, she realized with a sense of panic that he had never kissed her before—never, not even that night.... Her lips parted as her heart resumed its frantic pounding. Oh, God, what was she doing? She really knew so little about this man. She knew only that, like the fairy-tale creature who could spin gold from straw, Miles could pull a shocking lust from her unwitting body. Was that enough on which to build even a temporary marriage?

But the minister had said the fatal words, and the deed was done. The light-filled room seemed to dim around her as Miles's dark head lowered. Her vision blurred, and she clutched harder at his hand, groping for a reality reference. Just as her balance tipped, he swept out his other hand and pulled her to him. She sank against his hard chest gratefully.

But she didn't faint. Her eyes fluttered shut as his firm lips descended and, as the minister had instructed, boldly claimed her as his wife.

And then there was no need to faint. The mad marriage didn't need to make sense to her mind—it spoke eloquently to a more primitive logic. All struggle to understand was abandoned, and she was lost to any consciousness except warmth of those hard lips and the salty-sweet taste of his tongue between her teeth.

Subtly the kiss deepened, pressing further, demanding a response that her body was only too ready to deliver. Her mouth molded to his. Her arms rose up and over his broad shoulders, and her shaking palms cupped the rounded muscles under his shoulder blades. Her knees trembled and then seemed to disappear—she felt she existed only at those points that touched him, her hips, her breasts, her hands, her mouth.

If only she could have stayed there forever, floating in that timeless place. But someone—perhaps Tessa—chuckled happily in the distance.

"Wow," a voice whispered, and Miles drew away. The breeze blew across her wet lips, and it was cold.

It was over. Though she knew she must look shaken and blurred by the encounter, Miles looked as sardonic as ever. Tossing her an extremely unrepentant smile, he offered his arm with a caricature of chivalry.

"Shall we, Mrs. Anybody—I mean, Mrs. Hawthorne?"

As she met his scornful gaze, her heart exploded in a burst of pain. In that one cruel whispered sentence, he had made a mockery of the kiss, the ceremony, her foolish white dress, everything. What an idiot she had been to think, even for a moment, that his kiss meant anything. It was just his way of humiliating her, of establishing his dominance.

But everyone was watching. Tessa was crying, and even Evan looked misty-eyed. There was nothing to do but take Miles's arm, however gracelessly it had been offered, and turn to face the small congregation that had gathered to watch the ceremony, almost all of them people she didn't even know.

But one person was familiar. Her flustered gaze caught on a flushed, angry face, and her aching heart lurched in her breast.

It was Connie—in the back of the tiny church, clutching the pew in a knuckle-white grip. Darcy had never seen such a lovely face so transfigured by anger. Her blue eyes were hard and narrowed. Her rosebud lips were nearly invisible, clenched as they were against some almost ungovernable emotion.

Miles didn't so much as glance at Connie as they walked by, out to where the waiting car would take them back to Two Palms. But Darcy did. And then she saw the little boy who sat there with her. There was no anger on the little boy's face. Only about five years old, he clearly felt nothing but fidgety boredom. He was blond, like his mother, and attractive, with the charming, cocky self-absorption of all happy children. And yet, wasn't there something familiar about him? Something in the cockiness itself that she recognized?

But like a boat tugged along in a larger ship's wake, she was propelled past the child before she could put her finger on it. And then, in a shower of rice—Tessa's doing, of course—she followed Miles into the waiting car.

By SUNSET, Darcy felt she couldn't stand the deceit a moment longer. She had smiled and mouthed platitudes for almost three hours now. It was amazing how easily Tessa and Evan had fallen for the whole sentimental charade—true love at first sight, the whirlwind wedding, the happy ending. They'd made toast after toast during the small family dinner that was serving as a reception, and she had managed somehow to accept all the tributes with good grace. She only hoped that Mr. Stone would accept the marriage as easily.

But like a toy that had run out of batteries, she was losing energy for the game. She wanted to go upstairs, to her silent, comforting room and take off this wretched dress. If Miles put his arm around her one more time or dropped another false kiss on her ear, she would scream. What fun he was having, playing the role of the lucky bridegroom. It seemed to add to his enjoyment that she stiffened every time he touched her. He knew, of course, that it wasn't distaste that made her muscles rigid—it was her battle with desire.

"I think I'd better go to bed," she said, finally. "If I drink any more champagne, I just might fall asleep in my plate."

Rising politely, Miles gave her an intimate smile as he pulled out her chair.

"Well, that would never do," he said smoothly, ignoring Evan's boyish hoot of laughter. "Come on. We'll go together."

She blushed madly, her head spinning as she stood up far too fast. She had been sitting so long—and she had drunk so many glasses of champagne, accepting those ironic toasts. She held the back of the chair for balance.

"Oh, no," she said quickly, "there's no need. I'm just very tired...."

"Dar-cy!" Grinning, Tessa feigned horror. "You can't be *tired!*"

Even quiet Emily laughed at that, and the tension, the contrast between what everyone thought she was feeling and what she really was going through, was finally more than Darcy could stand.

"I certainly *can* be, and I *am,*" she said harshly, glaring at her younger sister. The grin fell from Tessa's lips with a crash, and Darcy was immediately penitent. Tessa hadn't deserved that. It was really Miles she wanted to scream at, not Tessa.

But she couldn't bring herself to apologize. The day had been emotionally grueling...and the night ahead might be worse.

She turned to Miles. "It's been a long day," she said meaningfully.

He put his hands on her shoulders and began to rub them, slowly, sensuously. "I know, sweetheart," he said, his voice as suggestive as the movements of his fingers. "I'll bet you could use a good massage, get rid of some of that tension...."

She tried to wriggle away, appalled by the way his fingers affected her. They might have been small electric prods, shooting currents through to her torso and into her midsection.

"Miles, I don't think—"

But his hands clamped down, the fingers hard against her collarbone.

"Yes," he said, and she heard the iron in his voice. "I think that's exactly what you need. Say good-night to everyone."

She gave in. "Good night," she said, trying to summon a smile, though the pressure of his fingers was hurting her. If there was going to be a scene, better to have it upstairs than down here, in front of Tessa and Evan and Emily... "See you in the morning."

"'Night," they called, and, his hands still on her shoulders, Miles maneuvered her up the stairs. They didn't speak, and she was glad of it—she was uncomfortably aware of the trusting trio they had left at the dining table below. Besides, she needed time to collect her thoughts. The champagne was making it difficult to think....

At the door to her room, she made as if to turn, but he held her straight.

"Not that one."

He marched her a few steps further down the hall and flung open another door—the door to his room.

Through the gaping doorway, she could see that the efficient maids of Two Palms had already moved her things in here. They had set out the only negligee she had that seemed appropriate for a wedding night—a nonsensical piece of pink froth. It lay like a stain across the bed.

It had seemed fine when she'd been thinking of Evan. But now the man lying at her side wasn't to be Evan. She had traded the safe, comfortable marriage she'd seen as a haven, for something much more terrifying—marriage to a man whose slightest touch could inflame desires she couldn't control.

And was he expecting to spend tonight with her, to watch her put on, and then take off, that gauzy pink gown? What about their decision that the "bargain" would be cleaner without sex?

Oh, she should have asked him about it—she should have made him promise. During the two weeks of rushed preparations, they had discussed her mother's will, George's legal rights, Tessa's schooling, the Hawthorne Industries stock prices—everything but their own personal plans. They had never once mentioned their sleeping arrangements, she realized with a sinking sense of doom. She'd never had the courage to bring up the subject, hoping only that he would leave things as they were.

Now she turned, her cheeks hot and her eyes questioning. "Here?"

"Yes," he said with a dark smile, his eyes glinting in the red and gold light from the sunset that poured through the picture window. And with a quick scoop he gathered her into his arms and carried her over the threshold.

Though she tried to hold herself apart, her body fit against his perfectly, her head seeking the hollow of his neck, her legs curling around his arms. And even over the pounding heartbeat that thrummed in her ears, she heard the door click softly shut behind them.

"Welcome home, Mrs. Hawthorne."

He eased her down slowly, letting her legs graze the hard length of him as they slid toward the floor. But when they touched the solid wood she could hardly feel it—she was numbed with confusion and desire. In the light from the setting sun, her white dress glowed as if made of claret, and Miles's eyes seemed filled with a bronze fire.

She didn't know what to say. The champagne was making her stupid.

But obviously he wasn't confused. The hot purpose in his eyes was almost frightening.

"Why don't you take this off?" His hands wandered to the satin-covered buttons that ran the length of her bodice. "It has served its purpose, don't you think?"

She stood quite still, almost unable to breathe, as, not waiting for her response, he slipped open the first two buttons. His hands were as golden as honey, their motion as fluid.

One by one the buttons slid free, until the lacy edge of her bra lay exposed. Soon it would be impossible to hide the desire that paralyzed her. Even now her breasts were puckering, swelling, straining against the rough lace that confined them.

Ashamed of this involuntary response, she grabbed his hand, stilling it before he could release the next button.

"No," she said, with effort. "This is a mistake."

"Is it?" His voice was low, and she shivered as if it had crossed the distance between them and dragged like a feather across her abdomen. "Are you sure?"

"Yes," she said, but the word lacked conviction. Her breath was coming hard again, heaving like the tide that lay just outside the window.

"Quite sure?" He stepped closer and ran his free hand lightly over her open lips, down her throat, to where a pulse beat in double time and, without further warning, into the open neck of her dress.

She gasped as his fingers slid under the satin, beneath the lace and found the warm skin of her breast. His hand cupped the gentle swell, and his two middle fingers settled themselves around the stiffened peak. The heat of his hand was almost unbearable as each deep, helpless breath she took pushed the curve of her breast against his palm.

"Are you?" His eyes held hers, and he watched her intently as his fingers rolled slowly together, rubbing the aching nipple until it was as hard as a hot pebble. Her focus blurred, and her lids lowered halfway over her unseeing eyes.

She was sure of nothing, nothing except that his touch was torture. His fingers pressed ever tighter, rolling the anguished tip of her breast harder, until it seemed to catch fire, and the fire shot through her body and down her legs. She moaned and leaned toward him, filling his hand.

"I don't know," she said, almost wildly. "I don't know..."

"Yes, you do." Releasing her, he yanked the rest of the buttons loose and pulled the fabric of her dress down, away from her shoulders, pinning her arms to her sides. He dragged the lace of the bra down, too, under the deep curve of her breasts and, with one hand at the base of her spine, bent her backward until her breasts lifted toward his mouth.

"You do know. You've known for a long time," he said, letting his lips brush the silken skin. "We both have."

And then his lips closed over her with hot demands, a fevered suckling that seemed to draw the strength easily from her body. Her head fell back, passion and alcohol making a wind-whipped chaos of her brain, so that all rational thoughts were whisked away, unformed, unreachable. His mouth was the only constant, his hot mouth and the small detonations of pleasure it set off inside her. She shut her eyes, letting the winds take her, going limp in his arms.

He was right. She had known for weeks that she needed this. It had been like the hurricane that even now still whirled in the Caribbean, just out of sight, not yet threatening them but holding in it the power to devastate whenever it chose to come closer. She'd tried not to think of the feelings Miles had churned up deep in her heart, had tried not to imagine the power this hopeless passion had to hurt her.

Her mind had denied the existence of the threatening storm, but her body had known. Her body had been trying to tell her, with its corkscrew of heat, its dull ache, its helpless midnight throbbing. It needed him, the total masculine power of him, the dark suckling of his mouth, the scalding imprint of his palms, the answering need that was burgeoning in him, insistent, pressing, refusing to be denied its home.

She felt that need now, hard against her, and without thinking she pressed toward it, as though to guide his passion. A small sound whispered past his lips, and he ran his hand up her spine and under her streaming hair, lifting her head.

"Open your eyes."

With great effort she did so and met his smoky brown gaze, as he watched her through lids that were as heavy with longing as her own. His lips were damp and swollen, and she longed to press them down against her breast again. Just beyond his dark head, the sunset was a low smoldering, a dense red core rimmed in the silver of approaching night. The same red, hot core burned inside her own body, the same silver sparkled across her skin, and she trembled in his arms.

"Tell me," he said, his voice low and compelling, his eyes boring into her. "Tell me how you feel."

Still she stared at him helplessly. How could she tell him? Were there words for this? Could anyone reduce this bewildering abandonment of self, this bottomless aching of need, to syllables and sentences?

"Empty," she said weakly, knowing the words were inadequate. "And . . . somehow lost."

Her voice trembled away, and with a moan he pulled her up, gathering her into the hard need of him, crushing her breasts against the stiff white of his shirt.

"You're not lost," he muttered fiercely against her hair. "You're mine."

His. The word sang into her heart. Yes—his. It was what she had felt today, when he'd put the beautiful ring on her shaking finger, when he had spoken the solemn words of promise. *His*.

She didn't protest when he carried her across the room, nor when he pressed her onto the bed, though the lace of her forgotten negligee bit into her bare back. She shut her eyes as, with sure but urgent hands, he pulled apart the remaining buttons of her dress, shoving the fabric aside impatiently, exposing her whole body to the glowing red light of the sunset.

The glow might have come from inside. He kissed her breasts slowly and let his lips slide down, around and up again, as though learning the shape of her. His hands slipped across her stomach, lingering briefly at each thrusting hipbone before disappearing into a place of sheer intensity, of blinding heat and shivering need.

Suddenly she was alive, swollen, burning. Every muscle was tensed, as though readied for a silent, motionless flight. She wasn't just a woman any more. She was a flaming globe, a golden hot balloon, tethered but straining, swelling up toward the freedom of the sky.

His hands and mouth urged her on, sent her blood speeding, heart galloping. Each touch was a gust of wind, pulling at her, teasing her toward release. Only the frailest, thinnest cord held her to the ground, and her body instinctively sought to sever the final thread. Her legs tightened; her head arched back. Her arms pushed at his shoulders in a delicious torment, as if to escape the relentless tug of the wind.

And then, with one last, expert pressure, the cord snapped, and she was free. Heat exploded through her—it was a conflagration that consumed all physical reality and sent her spinning through the black spaces. Nothing existed in that void but sensation, no awareness survived but the frightening ecstasy of release.

He held her until she found herself again, until she was a woman, a body, again. She felt his breath come unevenly against her cheek, and the muscles in the arms that held her shook. She knew his need was fierce.

She reached for him, suddenly eager to share the happiness she had found.

"Oh, Miles," she whispered, pressing her cheek against the pulse that throbbed in his neck, seeking the rhythm of the blood that coursed through him. "Miles, I do want you. I want you so much, and I—"

She stopped, her lips still touching the throbbing place in his neck. A cold shock thrust through her, freezing her voice, paralyzing her still half-open mouth. She couldn't go on. The word she had been about to say had stuck like a jagged rock in her throat, and it was jammed there, hurting her, refusing to be spoken or forgotten.

"What?" he asked, his swollen lips close to her ear. "You what?"

Blindly she shook her head, willing the word away, willing the terrifying thought away. "I—I don't know..."

His gaze darkened, and his hands slipped around to press against her bare back. "You what?" he repeated, insistent.

Did he know? Did he realize that she had been about to say that she loved him? She pressed her hands against his chest, trying to push free of him, trying to get far enough away to think clearly.

Oh, lord, how could she have allowed herself even to *think* such a thing? And was it true? Had she really been fool enough to *love* him?

The urge to flee was like a sizzling in her bones. It was too awful, too frightening, and she wanted to hide from the discovery. This was a three-year bargain, just the kind of simple contract businessmen like Miles signed over lunch. Love couldn't be considered, couldn't be spoken, couldn't even be *thought*.

But it *had* been thought. She had abandoned her body to him just as if theirs had been a real marriage, a true love.

Wriggling out of his embrace, she slithered a little bit away from him on the bed, struggling with the satin and lace, trying to cover her aching breasts. She didn't dare look at him, for fear he could read her new knowledge in her eyes, but he lay so still that she knew he was very, very angry. She didn't blame him. He wanted her badly—she wasn't naive enough to doubt that. And she had let him believe that he could have her, here in this room, right now, before the red sunset bled away completely.

Her hands shook as she fumbled with the satin buttons. She could hardly use the muscles in her hand—the corkscrew of desire ground through her, still demanding, still insisting. But she must never give her body what it asked for. If she did, she was lost indeed. If she let him into her body, he would enter her heart as well. And then she would love him hopelessly and forever.

She choked on the tears that pushed against her throat. But he was still waiting—he was like an ominous shadow beside her—and she *had* to say something.

"I was just going to say," she lied, "that I don't think we should let this happen. It would be...nice, I know, but it would be a bad mistake. It would complicate things so much, don't you see? And we had decided—hadn't we—that we didn't want things to get messy...."

Her voice trailed off as she summoned the courage to look at him. His face was gray, and she realized suddenly that the last remnant of sunset had been smothered by the descending night. Her dress, which only moments before had been incandescent with reflected light, was now a ghostly silver.

He laughed, a harsh sound, and she winced under its rasping. "Messy? Is that what you think of this?" He flicked a hand toward her nakedness as though disgusted.

He lurched up from the bed, away from her. Looking down at her with black eyes, he spoke roughly. "My God, what an accomplished tease you are, Darcy Skyler. And just a minute ago, I might have thought you—" He dismissed whatever thought he had with a harsh wave of his hand. "But to hell with that now. At least, thank heaven, I'm not the poor, heartbroken fool Evan was. Is this the way you caught him in your net—with these nasty little bait-and-switch games?" He didn't give her time to answer, his anger clearly driving him with a vicious whip. "Is this the thanks *he* would have received for riding to your rescue? Would you have turned *him* out of your bed with such transparent platitudes?"

A tease? Her body had been punishing her too much already. Now, under his unbridled, unfair contempt, she snapped. A button tore loose under her furious fingers, and she heard it clatter to the hardwood floor. Her beautiful dress, ruined... her wedding night the cruel farce she should have known it would be. She stood up rigidly.

"No," she threw back at him, her voice almost a keening. "No, I wouldn't have. If it had been Evan, I would have welcomed him, with gratitude."

"Gratitude?" He shot the word out like a poisoned arrow. "Payment would be a better term, wouldn't it? You were willing to sell your body to him for the price of a wedding ring, because that's the only thing he would have settled for."

"You don't know what you're talking about," she said, working to keep her voice low. Though her heart was breaking, the others must never know what misery lay behind these closed doors. Poor Evan, who felt so guilty already about letting her down. And, please, she told herself, swallowing her fury down hard, let Tessa, especially, continue to dream whatever teenaged dreams still danced in her head....

"Oh, I think I do." He spoke quietly, too, but it was a deadly quiet. His face might have been chiseled from granite, his features were so hard and silvered with moonlight. "You were prepared to make whatever bargain you had to make, with whoever was willing—"

"Well, what about you?" She hardly recognized the acid tones that came from her lips, but tears burned at her eyelids, and she had to speak harshly to cover the weakness. "Your motives were hardly philanthropic, were they? You don't give a tinker's damn about me, and you wouldn't have made this deal if it hadn't suited your purposes perfectly. You'll get your precious stock back, and you'll get your revenge on George, or whatever it is you want. I think that's plenty of payoff. Why in God's name should you get *me*, too?"

His eyes narrowed, as though she had hit him. He cursed once and strode to a side door and flung it open, revealing a sitting room beyond. He turned once more toward her, his handsome face marred by anger.

"Why indeed? You're cold, and calculating and the kind of tease I wouldn't have put up with in junior high school. So here's an even better question. Why in God's name should I *want* you?"

CHAPTER SEVEN

SHE STAYED in her room most of the day, unable to face anyone. By the time she dragged herself down to dinner, Tessa and Evan were already gathered on the back porch, drinks in hand. She didn't ask where Miles was, embarrassed to admit she didn't know.

"Hi," she said, turning toward the bar quickly, hoping Tessa wouldn't notice her shadowed eyes. She had used a clown's portion of blusher and eye makeup in an effort to give her face some color, but it probably wouldn't fool anyone. Perhaps, she thought with a good deal of irony, everyone would just think she had stayed awake late into the night, as brides often do, and then slept all day.

But even Tessa didn't seem curious—she just cocked her head toward Evan and grinned. Darcy gave Evan a quick glance—he stood with both elbows on the railing, staring into a cocktail glass that was nearly empty, lost in some charming dream of Emily.

Darcy plopped a couple of ice cubes into a small glass, dribbled in some scotch and, giving Tessa a lifted eyebrow, went to stand near him at the railing.

Sunsets must always be beautiful here, she thought. Tonight colors flew like flags across the sky, orange and peach, violet and gold and blue. A light wind ruffled her cotton T-shirt and blew the loose legs of her khaki shorts against her thighs. Hard to believe only twenty-four hours had elapsed since the sunset that had filled Miles's room ...

When after a couple of moments Evan still didn't speak, she nudged him with her elbow.

"Hey—are you with us? Or are you on that plane with Emily?"

He grinned. "Sorry. I guess I was. It already seems like she's been gone forever."

"I'll bet." She sipped her drink and balanced it on the railing. "Did you set the date?"

"Yep. August thirty-first. A whole month! I can't stand it." His face was glowing, and suddenly she felt about a hundred years older than he was. Such innocence! What would he have thought of the nasty scene in Miles's bedroom last night?

"Well, wonderful weddings take a while to plan," she said patiently, stirring her drink with her finger. Maybe if she had a couple of drinks, she'd be able to make it through dinner. Maybe she'd even be able to eat. Right now she felt she might never eat again. Food would just never make it past the glacier of ache around her heart.

"Yeah, I guess." Then he smiled. "Your wedding didn't take that long, and it was nice. And now you're finally rid of George The Third."

"Ummm." She smiled, remembering the nickname she had given George when he arrived, stepfather number three. . . .

"You know, Darcy." Evan's voice was low. "I always kind of thought I'd be the guy who rescued you from George."

Darcy reached up and put a kiss on his cheek. "I know," she said softly. "But now that you've met Emily, aren't you glad you didn't have to?"

He grinned, obviously unable to deny it. "Well," he said, putting his arm around her. "It all worked out for the best after all, didn't it? You and Miles, me and Emily. Who ever would have thought it?"

Who indeed? But Darcy didn't voice her sense of irony. She just relaxed into the companionable embrace.

"You do like her, don't you, Darcy?" He was pitifully eager for her approval. He took her hand and squeezed it. "You don't think I let you down? I know I said I'd always be here for you, but it all happened so fast. And you never did give me any hope, you know."

He frowned, and his sweet brown eyes searched her face. "You do understand, don't you? I was going to write you, really, right away, but then all of a sudden you were already here. It was amazing how it happened so suddenly for both of us. I guess the real thing comes like that sometimes." He winked conspiratorially. "I guess you know that just as well as I do."

Her face paled under the brave makeup. If only it *had* been true—if only she had married for innocent, imperative love, had spent last night in the arms of a man who adored her. . . .

And then, without warning, the glacier around her heart was melting—her chest was swollen with the pressure, and her eyes were brimming with a salty overflow. She couldn't speak, so she just put out her hand in a gesture of understanding and forgiveness. Evan's hand met hers, and their fingers locked.

"Hello, all." The voice that broke the silence was like a cold wind, and she felt the glacier reforming, stiffening into a solid mass of pain surrounding her heart. Miles stood in the doorway, his hands tight around the edge of the sliding glass pane, his eyes riveted to the spot where the two of them stood, hands entwined.

For a horrible moment shame stained her cheeks, as if she had been caught in an indiscretion. She tried to pull away from Evan, but her body didn't seem to be under her jurisdiction, and it wouldn't move. She couldn't even speak.

But Evan obviously suffered no such embarrassment. "Hi, Miles," he said. "Pull up a chair. There's still plenty of ice left."

"No, thanks," Miles responded dryly. "There's nothing here I want."

Too caught up in his own happiness to catch nuances, Evan squeezed Darcy's hand once lightly and then moved away. "Emily's gone home, you know. Wedding gown fittings and all that."

Miles nodded. "I heard. Buck up, Ev. She's worth the wait." Turning his icy gaze to Darcy, he smiled coldly. "It's too bad Emily had to leave, isn't it? But I know you'll do all you can to keep Evan from getting lonely."

What was he implying? That she was making a play for Evan? Good God, what a mind! Well, she wasn't going to spend the next three years listening to his insulting innuendoes, either in the bedroom or over the dinner table.

Pressing the heels of her hands against the edge of the railing, she faced him.

"Listen, Miles—"

"Oh, Darcy—that reminds me," Tessa broke in. "George called while you were asleep."

"He *did?*" Darcy splashed scotch and water across her bare leg as she lurched forward. "Oh, Tess, why didn't you tell me?"

The news upset her more than she would have expected it to. What could George do to her now that she was safely married? And yet his name made an ugly sound, a discordant chord.

Miles stepped between them. "It's okay, Tessa. I told the lawyer where you and Darcy were, and he probably told George. It's nothing to worry about. Just tell us what he said."

Shifting her weight slightly toward the last rays of the sun, Tessa wrinkled her brow. "I don't know. I was out playing tennis with Brad. Alice took the message." A hint of discomfort lurked in her eyes as she met Miles's strangely sympathetic gaze. "I guess I wanted to forget about it, really. I know he's going to be mad at us for not telling him where we went, and..." She looked away toward the Gulf. "And about the wedding and...and everything."

Darcy tried to smile. "That's silly, Tess," she said. She brushed irritably at the sparkling droplets of scotch that lay on her tanned thigh. "Now that Miles and I are married, it doesn't really matter if George is mad or not. I explained to you about Mother's will. Skyler Stores belongs to us now."

Tessa sighed. "Yeah. But he's going to be mad about that, too."

Frustrated, Darcy looked back toward the Gulf. How could she convince Tessa when she could only half convince herself? Would everything really be fine now? She twisted the ring around her finger, pressing its intricate flowers against her fingertips, and wished it all were simpler.

But Tessa had lost interest in George already and had begun arguing with Evan about the virtues of eloping. Miles joined Darcy at the railing.

"Stone says you can call a board meeting in about three weeks," he said quietly. "It'll take him that long to draw up all the papers and of course, though he didn't mention this, to look into my credit rating. To see if I'm just after your pretty portfolio."

Ignoring Miles's sarcasm, she turned toward him gratefully. Only three weeks! Three weeks and George would *have* to leave her alone. Some of the oppression that had weighed so heavily on her heart lifted. Nothing mattered except that she and Tessa were finally free of George....

Free. The word sounded so good. She'd waited a long time, given up so much, to be able to say it.

"Thank you, Miles. That was very nice of you," she said, but the smile dropped from her lips as she met his expression. Cold.

"You didn't think I'd forget the purpose of our union so soon, did you, Mrs. Hawthorne?" His voice was lazily sarcastic. "Especially when you make it so clear there could be no other purpose."

Darcy glanced quickly to where Tessa and Evan were laughing.

"They'll hear you," she warned.

"Oh, dear," he said with elaborate insincerity. "We certainly mustn't disillusion our dear Evan."

She pulled in an angry breath. "Miles, don't start—"

"Don't start what? Telling the truth? Why not?" His eyes were black, and the indolent tone was gone from his voice. "I think this marriage could use a little honesty. And..." His voice deepened to a profound disdain. "And at least I don't start things I don't intend to finish.'"

She flushed, as much from resentment as from embarrassment. She hadn't started that scene last night, and he very well knew it! But with Evan and Tessa so near there was no chance to reply in kind. So she contented herself with raising her brows loftily, and turned away as haughtily as she could.

"I think I'll go for a walk along the beach," she said, loudly, setting her glass, still nearly full, on the table.

Tessa looked shocked. "But, Darcy, dinner—"

"I'll be back for dinner," she called, tripping quickly down the wooden steps that led to the beach. Both Tessa and Evan were urging her to stay, but Miles's voice was noticeably silent. "I'll be back. I promise."

But half an hour later she had gone so far down the beach she knew she'd never make it back to Two Palms in time for dinner. And she wasn't sure she wanted to. She'd finally calmed down, and she hated to return to the battlefield.

It was a perfectly marvelous evening, with a full moon like an overturned pitcher of milk pouring light onto the white sand. The air was cool, and the rhythmic push and pull of the waves was restful. Out here she could almost forget about Miles. . . .

So why go back? Why not just keep walking? Back there, so many things confused her. Miles confused her, and in truth, she confused herself. Even when Miles was being unkind to her, she was painfully conscious of his sensuality. Her body reacted to his as though it had been programmed to do so and was beyond conscious control. Damn! She kicked a broken piece of driftwood out of her way. She had married to *gain* control of her life— not lose it.

But she had to go back. Tessa would worry. Reluctantly she turned around, savoring her last few minutes of peace. High summer was popular on Sanibel Island. Sounds of laughter drifted to her from the condominiums, from the cottages and even, occasionally, from other passing strollers.

She had almost made it back to Two Palms when she saw them. It was the little boy's high-pitched laughter that drew her attention. He sounded so happy. So alive, so confident...

She saw them immediately. Standing at the water's edge, looking out over the milky Gulf, their handsome, trim silhouettes made a charming tableau. The small, lovely lady, her blond hair glowing in the moonlight. The tall, powerful man, and the little boy who rode astride his shoulders and laughed at the vast water below him.

She didn't doubt for an instant that it was Miles. So it was no surprise when the trio turned around and walked toward the street. She saw his features clearly. He was smiling as he had never smiled at her.

Above him, the little boy wore a red baseball cap, cocked sideways on his blond head, and he'd folded his small arms across Miles's broad forehead for stability. He was grinning, too. Connie walked close alongside, one hand up and wrapped around the boy's bare foot. It was a moment of such naked intimacy, both physical and emotional, that Darcy felt like an intruder. She prayed they wouldn't see her.

Another trill of laughter, this time Connie's silver tones, floated on the cool night air as their shadowy forms disappeared into the shrubbery that grew along the Hawthorne's pool. And then, as if it had all been a movie that, once ended, had faded to black, Darcy was alone.

She stood motionless for so long that her feet sank deep into the cool sand and the incoming waves bubbled around her ankles. So Miles was missing dinner, too, she thought irrelevantly. Or was he eating with Connie and her little boy? Her mind conjured up a picture of honeyed domesticity—spaghetti and laughter and just one more bedtime story.

And then, though she had not known she was going to, and though she had no idea why she did so, she wept.

"I'M NOT SUPPOSED to tell you this," Tessa said, hooking her arms over the small white kickboard and floating slowly through the blue water of the pool. Her wet hair gleamed like a garnet in the bright sunshine. "Evan made me promise not to. But he doesn't understand. He's just a man. It would take a woman to understand that you've just *got* to know."

What? Darcy's heart tightened almost imperceptibly, and she swam a few more strokes before answering. What could it be? It sounded troubling...it sounded like something she might not want to know.

"You shouldn't break a promise, Tess," she said, hating herself for the preachy tone. But she didn't want to hear any secrets. Some things should be left unsaid.

Especially the hateful, hurtful things—like the things she and Miles had said the other night. It was the night she had seen him with Connie on the beach. She'd planned to feign sleep, but by the time he finally came home, long after midnight, she'd been so wrought up she hadn't been able to control herself.

"Where have you been?" She knew she sounded like a shrewish fishwife, but she couldn't help it. She sat rigidly in bed, her hair tangled from her tossing and turning, and her hands clenched tightly in her lap.

"Out." He turned away from the closet long enough to give her a cold look and then returned to unbuttoning his shirt. "With friends."

"Until this hour?" Her voice was high and thin, like the sound of a spring being overwound, and her knuckles were milky white.

He shrugged his shirt off. "I saw no reason to hurry home."

His blank monotone was maddening, and she suddenly wanted to slap that poker player's mask from his features. She wanted him to fight back, to show that she meant something—anything—to him. She was, after all, his wife. How could he be so indifferent?

"Oh, really? Well, I suppose you had no trouble finding someone to be with whose company is more... enjoyable."

He disappeared into the blackness of the walk-in closet without answering, and she bit her lip until it stung. The silence dragged on until she finally said acidly, "Well, did you?"

He emerged, wearing only a thick black terry robe that grazed his strong legs just below the knees.

"Did I find someone? As a matter of fact I did. But what the hell difference does it make to you?" He leaned against the doorway and gave her an appraising look. "Why do you care?"

She couldn't immediately think of a response, so she just stared at him mulishly, wishing intensely that the sight of him didn't disorient her so. As though enjoying her confusion, he sauntered toward her, his strong, hair-darkened chest visible beneath the robe.

He sat on the edge of the bed and pulled the white satin covers down, exposing the pink chiffon of her gown. An unpleasant smile tweaked the corner of his mouth.

"Well? Why do you care whose company I enjoy?"

She pulled the covers higher over her breasts with stiff fingers. "I don't." She lifted her chin.

He put his hand beneath her jaw. "Really? Then why did you wait up for me?" He stroked the sensitive skin of her throat. "Had you perhaps changed your mind about being...enjoyable yourself?"

Anger stabbed her. What a patronizing tone! She swatted his hand away. "Hardly!" She was breathing heavily against the pain under her ribs. "It's just that we haven't passed the lawyer's test yet, and I would hate for your—your catting around to jeopardize our plans. There's too much at stake."

His jawline grew hard, and his brown eyes blackened. "Always got your eye on the main issue, haven't you?" He took her chin again between thumb and forefinger, but this time he squeezed it hard. "You've got a sweet face, angel, but you're as heartless as the computer that spits out my bank balance. Is it any wonder I was in no hurry to come home?"

She met his bitter gaze with stony pride. "In that case, I'm surprised that you came back at all."

"So am I," he spat back, pushing her chin away as though it repelled him. "So am I."

But he did come back, every night. Every night they lay, side by side, so close she could feel his body heat, and yet as distant as if they were on two separate continents.

He slept. She knew that from his slow, heavy breathing. She wanted sometimes to turn over and study his face, to see what he looked like in sleep, with the bitterness erased from his features. But she was afraid to turn around, afraid that he might catch her watching him. And so she just lay there, curled into herself, facing the window until the pink sun came up and she finally fell asleep, too.

Some marriage. Well, what had she expected? What adolescent fantasy had lurked behind her supposedly pragmatic decision to marry Miles Hawthorne? She couldn't let herself explore her heart on this issue.

"Are you even listening to me, Darcy?"

Tessa's voice was petulant and, coming to, Darcy dove briefly under the cool water in an effort to escape her thoughts. But naturally she had to surface again, and the sun beat down mercilessly on her shoulders just as the truth beat mercilessly against her brain.

"Good grief, it's hot," she said, trying to change the subject. She cupped water in her hands and splashed it across her face. "We should be inside, taking a siesta." She stared up into the blinding blue of the sky. "The hurricane may head this way after all. Evan says it's always hotter right before a hurricane."

"Oh, don't try to distract me," Tessa complained. "The hurricane has been stalled around Cuba forever, and nobody seems to know where it's heading anyhow. I hate all those coordinates."

Thus blithely dismissing the forces of nature and Darcy's scruples, Tessa lifted her feet up to inspect her newly painted toenails. "And anyhow I'm *going* to tell you, so don't try to go all bossy on me."

Darcy sighed, recognizing defeat. "All right," she said, perching on the pool steps and wringing the water out of the ends of her hair. "Tell."

"Okay." Tessa paddled over, still dangling from her little board. "Get this. Evan is going to throw a party for you."

For a minute Darcy just stared. This innocent piece of gossip was so far from the dark skeletons she had feared. Or was it a blond skeleton? Then she laughed, at her own macabre image, at her own foolish paranoia. How could Tessa have found out about Connie? There might not even be anything to find out.

"A party? For me?"

"For you and Miles, because you didn't get a real reception when you got married. A party for the *newlyweds*." Tessa laughed, too, enjoying the romantic sound of the word. "Evan wants it to be a surprise, but I know you need a new dress, so I thought I'd better tell you. But you'd better never let on that you know."

"Does Miles know?"

"Nope." Tessa looked pleased. "And you'd better not tell him. No pillow talk or anything."

As if there were any chance of that! "I won't," Darcy assured her, hoping her cheeks hadn't changed color. Sometimes she wished fervently that she and Miles hadn't agreed to pretend the marriage was a normal one. In addition to making Mr. Stone's approval more likely, it had also seemed the easiest way—for poor Evan's conscience, for Tessa's dreams and for any possible legal loopholes George might be hunting for. And yet those nights lying silently by Miles's side were so painful....

"I won't breathe a word," she said again, to cover her embarrassment. "When is it going to be?"

"Saturday," Tessa whispered, screwing up her face and making head-pointing gestures toward the other end of the pool. "Shhh! Careful!"

Darcy looked, wondering what had caused such an abrupt change of Tessa's tone, and her heart thudded once, hard, against her breast. She clutched at the hot silver rail that ran along the steps. It was Miles.

What was he doing here during the day? He was *never* here at this hour. He had stopped at the far edge of the pool, looking equally surprised to find her there.

Dressed only in navy swimming trunks he looked almost unreal, like a photograph advertising a tropical holiday. His skin was too honey maple to seem real, his body too perfectly sculpted, his shoulders too wide, his hips too narrow, his legs too strong. Even the scene looked artificial. The hibiscus behind him was too pink, the sky too blue, the smokestack clouds too white, the palms too gently ruffling in a breeze too balmy.

Certainly it was too ironic that she should have worn her foolish bikini today. She cursed the impulse that had made her do it, even though her only other suit was still wet from a morning swim. Would it have hurt to put on a wet suit just once?

"Hi, Miles," Tessa called, shoving her kickboard away and climbing quickly up the steps. "I was just leaving. I was telling Darcy I was in desperate need of a siesta, but she simply *would* not give up the idea of a swim. Come on in. You can keep her company and give her the latest hurricane coordinates."

Darcy could have pinched her sister's saucy ankle as she went by. What a fib! But she knew Tessa had meant well—"the newlyweds" and all that—and now she was stuck. She managed a polite smile in Miles's direction.

"Hi," she said, her voice abnormally high. "Were you planning to swim?"

He nodded, accepting a quick hug from Tessa as she scooted by. Funny, Darcy thought, as a tiny pin seemed to prick at her heart, that Tessa could hug him so easily, while she, his wife, would have found the gesture perfectly impossible....

"Yes, I was." He tilted his head, and the sun caught the strong line of his jaw. "Is that a problem?"

"Of course not." She felt like a child accepting a dare. I can do it...you don't scare me... Her back stiffened, and her jaw set firmly, though she made her voice as casual as she possibly could. "I'd be delighted."

She intended to maintain a total indifference, but she couldn't take her gaze from him as he climbed the steps to the long, blue diving board. He walked out to the edge of the platform and raised his arms above his head. In that position, with his shoulders spread and his feet locked together, his body was a perfect triangle, and the sunlight poured over him like a spotlight, as though nature itself paused to watch the extraordinary spectacle.

There was barely a splash as he dove, from fingertips to toes a flawless line. The water seemed to open for his entry and then to close greedily around him. Her breath caught in her throat. He really was so very gorgeous, so very sensual. Who could be indifferent to that?

She was still on the steps—like a sitting duck—when he surfaced. He shook his lush hair vigorously, but glittering drops still nestled among his thick lashes. His shoulders cleared the water as he walked toward her, then his broad chest, and up until she could just glimpse the dark band of his swim suit at the narrowest point of his waist.

Why wasn't he speaking? Why was he just staring at her with that deep brown gaze? "It's really hot," she said, smiling brightly, "isn't it?" Oh, lord, how absurd. What could have possessed her to say that, of all things?

But only the smallest corner of his wide mouth even twitched. "Do you think so?" He studied her. "You do look a little flushed. Maybe you should get out of the sun. It may be a bit much for you."

"I can handle it," she countered with a touch of asperity. He needn't think she would be overcome by the sight of a man's bare chest, no matter how broad and well muscled it was. She wasn't *that* susceptible.

"Good." He leaned one elbow against the coping and watched her. "So, was Tessa telling you about Evan's surprise party?"

Her jaw dropped slightly. "She said you didn't know!"

"Oh, I don't, officially," he said. "But it's pretty hard to put together a big party around here without my getting wind of it somehow."

She nodded. That had occurred to her, too. "It's very nice of Evan," she said stiltedly.

"Yes. He's very nice. Unfortunately, he's also very naive."

She slid her hand nervously across the wet metal of the railings. "What do you mean?"

"I mean that he quite believes our marriage is something to celebrate. He told me just the other day how lucky I am. I don't think it has ever once occurred to him that you're the coldest wife a man ever had."

CHAPTER EIGHT

SATURDAY CAME so quickly. She wasn't ready, and as eight o'clock approached she felt a childish urge to run away. How could she face a houseful of people who would come to celebrate this farce that was her marriage? She knew it would call for an elaborate charade of happiness, for a false show of intimacy that would slash at her heart even while she smiled.

So until now she hadn't even let herself think about the party, and the days had flown by. Most of them had been spent dragging along behind Tessa, looking for the perfect dress.

Finally they found it. It was so simple she almost hadn't noticed it on the rack, but when she tried it on she barely recognized herself. Even with the stunning Tessa standing next to her, she knew she looked beautiful. Her bare shoulders rose from a heart-shaped silk bodice, and a black velvet belt emphasized her slim waist before the skirt spilled, full and flowing, all the way to the floor.

And the marvelous dusky pink color! Ashes of roses, the saleslady had called it, and Darcy had decided the term was most appropriate for this occasion. But, irony aside, the color did flatter her, finding highlights in her hair that she had never suspected, and throwing a rosy glow over her tanned skin.

The dress hung now on the hook over her bathroom door. She'd had her bath, but she couldn't quite bring herself to fix her hair and put on her makeup. Instead she sat, wrapped only in a white towel, on the edge of the big, lonely bed and stared at the dress. It seemed to belong to someone else.

A light rap sounded on the door to the sitting room, but before she could rouse herself to answer it, the knob twisted and the door flew open.

"Darcy? I need to talk to you," Miles began, his gaze going instinctively toward the vanity, where he probably expected her to be sitting, putting the final touches to her makeup. When he didn't find her there, his eyes swept the room, coming to rest abruptly at the bed.

"Darcy—"

His voice simply stopped, as if it was a faucet that had been wrenched shut. A darkness clouded his face, and his hands slowly clenched into white-knuckled fists at his side.

Was it anger? Her gaze darted to the clock on the bedside table. She wasn't *that* late, was she?

"I'm sorry I'm not ready," she said, her tongue strangely thick and causing her to stumble over her words. She stood up slowly, trying to tuck the end of the towel deeper into the fold so that it wouldn't wiggle loose. She felt so very naked under it, under those dark eyes that were wordlessly devouring her.

And without her permission, her body was responding. What had moments before been the thick softness of the towel was suddenly rough against her sensitive breasts. What had been adequate coverage was suddenly frighteningly insufficient. She could feel the ends of the towel separating around her thighs, could sense the rim cupping just below the curve of her buttocks.

Perhaps it wouldn't have felt so strange if he had been in disarray as well. But he was so crisp and elegant in his black tuxedo, so formal, so armored, compared to her intense vulnerability. Somehow the comparison made her feel ashamed, and she struggled to control her body's response.

"You wanted to talk to me?"

At the sound of her stiff voice he seemed to shake himself from the stupor and, looking studiously away, found words again. "Yes, I did. I wanted to warn you that we've had another call from George. He heard about the party. Apparently some of the people Evan invited know George, too, so they probably mentioned it. Anyhow, he's planning to be here."

He walked to the vanity and shoved aimlessly at the cosmetics cluttered there, not looking in her direction. "I just thought you should know."

She sank back onto the bed, her knees weak. George! Any audience for tonight's performance would have been disturbing enough, but George!

Her lips trembled as she voiced her fears. "What do you think he wants?"

"I don't know." He looked at her in the mirror, as though only at one remove did he trust himself to do so. "Maybe he just wants to try to make friends, make amends. You do hold the purse strings now, you know."

She shook her head, running her fingers through her long, uncombed hair. "That's not his way. He—he's here to cause trouble. I know it." Suddenly her fingers were wobbly, and she dropped them to her lap. "Oh, God..."

"He can't cause any trouble here. You know that."

But she couldn't answer. Her throat felt swollen shut. She didn't feel ready to meet George. Her marriage was so empty, her heart so miserable, that she felt sure George would see it in her eyes. And he mustn't ever know. If he knew, he'd find a way to get the stock—and Tessa.

She nodded blindly, vehemently. "Yes, he can," she choked. "He can. He's going to be furious. He's here to hurt us. I *know* he is."

"Well, he can't." Miles sounded exasperated. "What can he do? Let him rave if he wants to. He can't change anything."

"You don't know him," she said, and she couldn't stop her voice from shaking. Tears were pushing at the back of her eyes. "Y-you don't know how dangerous he is."

Miles turned around slowly and watched her for a long minute before answering.

"Dangerous?"

She heard the surprise in his voice, but she nodded stubbornly. Of course he was surprised. No one had ever really seen through George.

"You're...afraid of him, aren't you?" He put the question quietly, as though the idea had just occurred to him and he was thinking out loud.

She folded her arms across her chest and ducked her head. "Yes."

"Why?" His voice was rough, bewildered. "Hatred I can understand—but why fear?"

She shook her head helplessly. "I don't know if I can explain it."

He didn't prompt her, but his silence was expectant, waiting.

"For so long, George has stood for everything that was wrong with my life," she said finally, wondering why she was even trying. She hadn't ever talked about this to anyone—why now, to this man who above all others had the power to hurt her?

"My mother wasn't a silly woman," she went on. "But she was different after my father died. She seemed to need attention desperately. She was lonely, I know, but she behaved so...foolishly."

She didn't look at him, afraid she might see something in his expression that would stop the words. Her voice was stronger now. "She married three times after my father. Three times. Each one was worse than the last—until finally she sank low enough for George."

She stared at the dusky pink dress. Ashes of roses. She could almost smell them in the room now.

"I loved my mother," she said slowly, "but I was ashamed. I was only sixteen when she married George, but even I could see what kind of man he was. He drank. He...he wasn't ever faithful to her. There were lots of women. I'd hear them talking at the club. And then—" Her voice broke slightly, but she had to go on. She'd come this far; she had to finish. She squeezed her hands together, struggling for composure. She *wanted* to finish. "And then, just before my seventeenth birthday, he decided he wanted me."

She sensed a violent movement at the dressing table, and something metallic clattered to the floor.

"No—" Miles's voice was strangled.

"Yes," she said, watching her fingers as they knitted in and out of one another, white knuckles threading pink skin. "It was just little things at first. A kiss that missed my cheek and caught my lips. A hug that lasted too long. Coming in to 'tuck' me in bed...."

"Why didn't you tell your mother?"

"I did. She was furious. She said I'd never wanted her to marry anyone after my father, that I wasn't willing to let her go on living...."

Tears had found their way into her eyes and were pooling there, drowning out her vision of the room. But she forced herself to talk on. "But that wasn't why, of course. She just didn't want to see. And then, then..."

The tears were flowing now, from an inexhaustible, silent spring. They ran down her cheeks and spilled onto her hands.

"And then what?" Miles hadn't moved, but his voice was harsh, urgent. "What did he do?"

"He tried—" She couldn't go on now. "He tried to force me—"

And suddenly Miles was kneeling before her, his body pressing between her shaking knees, his hands on her shoulders. "My God, Darcy," he murmured, running his hands up her neck and into the back of her hair. He pulled her toward him, burying his face in her throat. "I'm so sorry."

And somehow his touch gave the strength she needed to finish. "I stopped him," she said, her voice steadier. "He was drunk, horribly drunk, and a beer bottle had fallen on the floor between us. I picked it up, and I hit out at him. I cut him—on the temple, just above his eye. There was blood everywhere. I was afraid I had killed him...."

He looked up, his eyes bottomless and black. "I wish you had."

"No," she said, closing her eyes to blot out the memory of the blood. "I don't know what he told my mother, but he never came near me again after that. But he hated me, hated me desperately for humiliating him.

And ever since my mother died he's been trying to get his revenge.''

He frowned. "The poker games?"

Nodding, she swallowed hard, remembering that Miles himself had been one of the poker boys.

"But I didn't care about that. They were just boys. I could handle them." She laughed hollowly. "The last one I chased away with a gun."

A smile touched his lips. "A beer bottle *and* a gun. You're a dangerous woman. Why did you decide you had to run away? It doesn't sound to me as if you needed a husband to protect you."

She didn't answer the smile, looking past him toward the pretty party dress Tessa had picked out for her. "It was because of Tessa."

"Tessa?" He looked bewildered.

She put her hands over her face, covering the tears that threatened to flow again. "He had started with Tessa," she said, her voice smothered by her wet palms. "Just, oh, just saying things that had double meanings, just looking with that awful look—but I knew where it would lead. I had to do something. She was so young, even younger than I had been because she's been so much more protected than I was."

He stared at her for a moment. "Oh, my God," he said. "I didn't know."

"No one knew," she said bitterly. "He seems so—so plausible. Most people think George is just a wonderful fellow. That's how he gets away with it."

He frowned. "What about the police? They know how to deal with men like that."

She shook her head violently. "No. What could I have said? That he *looked* at my sister funny? It would always have been my word against his, and he's so damnably smooth. And what would have become of Tessa even if they *had* believed me? I couldn't be sure they'd let her live with me."

She looked at him, her eyes burning. "And, you see, then Tessa would have known. She would have had to know—to think about things so vile... And nothing could take that knowledge, that ugly, horrible knowledge, away from her. I won't have Tessa living with that. No child should have to—"

"No," he said, touching her face, "no child should have to."

His fingers found a weakness deep inside her, and once again tears lay heavy under her eyelids. "So, you can see, can't you, that it wasn't the company at all. It was just that if I could do anything, anything, to protect her, I had to do it."

A curious look altered his features, and she felt rather than saw him draw back. "Including sacrificing yourself in marriage to a man you didn't love?"

"Yes." One of the tears seeped out and ran down her cheek, only to detour around his fingers. "Even that." She looked up, her eyes pleading for understanding. "But I would have tried to make him happy, Miles. I wouldn't have sacrificed his happiness, too."

For a grinding instant his hand tightened on her face, and then he dropped his arm and rose to his feet.

"I'm sorry," he said, his voice as taut as reins pulled against a bolting horse. "I'm really very sorry."

He walked away slowly, toward the door to the sitting room. "I didn't know how complicated all this was for you." He paused at the doorway, his body rigid, his hand white around the doorknob. "I shouldn't have said the things I said. And I certainly never should have..."

He seemed at a loss for words and raked his hand through his hair. Finally he laughed, a short, bitter sound. "God, you must have thought you'd traded one nasty, groping lecher for another."

"Oh, no, Miles!" She rose to her feet, holding out her hands. "It hasn't been like that at all."

"No?" His eyes were hooded. "I was trying to force you, wasn't I, in my own way?"

She stepped toward him blindly. "No, of course you weren't." She grabbed his arm. "You weren't trying to make me do anything I didn't want to do."

"Oh, yes I was," he said, his bitter eyes locking with hers. "I was trying to make you want me the way I wanted you...trying to make you need me so badly you couldn't say no."

"But I already did," she cried, pressing her hands against his chest, not caring how foolish the admission was. She couldn't let him believe she thought of him as another George. She loved him too much.

Loved him. The word was like a burning, and she closed her eyes to feel its brand. She could no longer deny it, not even to herself. That was why she'd wanted to tell him about George—because she loved him, more than she had ever expected to love a man, and she wanted to share the truth with him. She wanted him to understand her, perhaps even forgive her a little.

Maybe he would never love her, maybe Connie already held that place in his heart, but Darcy was his wife, at least for a little while, and she wanted to know him as a wife.

"I already wanted you," she said again, opening her eyes and turning their pleading depths toward his. "I want you now."

A muscle twitched in his jaw, and his hand grew whiter around the knob. "You don't have to say this, Darcy. In spite of the way I've acted, I'm not really another George. I'll leave you alone."

But she knew by the heat that rose from his body that he was lying. He wanted her, too.

"Yes, I do," she said. "I *do* have to say it." She pried his fingers from the metal knob and guided his hand to the place where her heart pounded against her breast. "This is why."

At first his hand was stiff with his resistance but as she guided it inside the white cotton that covered her breast, with every inch his fingers grew more supple, as if the heat of her breast had thawed them. The tucked-in ends of the towel began to give way as the fabric stretched to accommodate his hand, and finally it dropped, falling at her feet like a snowdrift.

She heard a quick intake of breath as his eyes ran over her nakedness. "Don't . . ."

"I have to," she said, and she did. Her body was coiling into a knot of desire so thick and twisted she could hardly stand. "I need you, Miles. Show me—teach me what real passion is like."

Disbelief raced through his eyes as he stared at her. But something he saw there, in the deep brown of her eyes, made him believe, and he pulled her to him with a small cry of triumph.

"Oh, Darcy." His hands tangled in her hair as he tilted her head back. "It can be so beautiful. What a man and a woman can be together is the most wonderful thing in the world. I could kill him for trying to take that away from you."

His hands were so tight the skin of her cheeks stretched back, but she tried to smile. "He didn't," she whispered. "He didn't take anything. And now I want to give it to you."

"Darcy." His voice was thick, his eyes dilated, just black coals rimmed in a burning brown fire. His hands traveled down her neck, across the shivering length of her spine and over the gentle curve of her hips. At the top of her thighs they stopped, and he raised her off the ground.

"Come." A slight pressure told her what he wanted. Her legs lifted and spread, locking behind him, and her arms wrapped around his neck.

His hands held her tightly, pressing her to him as they took the one, two steps—only two steps, but they were agony to her as his clear need intensified her own—and reached the bed. Slowly, as though reluctant to release her, he lay her against the satin covers.

And then, pulling away, he stood beside her, slowly removing his own clothes.

The black silky ribbon of his tie was the first to fall to the floor, followed by the black puddle of his jacket, the white flag of his shirt. And then the rest of his clothes disappeared as well, leaving only a pure masculinity that took her breath away.

The overhead light burned brightly, its crystals sparkling over him, revealing a body so lean, so powerful, that her hands crept instinctively to her stomach, palms pressing hard against the flat valley between her hipbones, seeking to touch the ache that tormented her.

"Hurry," she whispered. Not enough breath remained in her constricted chest for her to speak the word aloud. She was afraid she might coil so tightly into herself that she would spiral away into nothingness.

"No, sweetheart," he said, kneeling beside her on the bed. "You must never hurry a miracle."

The word was not an exaggeration. She closed her eyes and watched in a haze of desire as he created a rainbow of colors inside her. The mist-green sensuality that engulfed her like a wet, primal forest. The seeping, pulsing blood-pink throb as his hands massaged her breasts. The blinding vermillion as his lips closed over the stiffened nipples. The shimmering silver that rose up through her like sparkling smoke when his fingers strayed between her legs. The deep violet ache that grew more swollen inside her with each circle his fingers traced, until it filled her from thigh to throat.

"Make love to me, Miles," she said, surprised that she could still talk. But the glowing colors would not be ignored.

His breath was ragged as he lowered himself over her, his strong arms rising like ribboned columns from either side of her neck.

"It will hurt a little," he said thickly. "I'm sorry."

She reached up and pulled his strong thighs down toward her. "I'm not," she said. "I want to feel everything."

The pain flew in and out of her consciousness like the absent prick of a thorn just before you smell the rose. And then she wrapped her legs again around his back, and she felt his muscles moving rhythmically under her calves. Her body began to match the movements, and she knew just a heartbeat before it happened when he was going to quicken the pace. Slowly, a grace note at a time, the tempo increased, until her head grew light and every atom of her awareness was focused on the spot where their bodies fused together.

And then he was filling her with every color at once, colors that flashed and sparked and raced through her blood, exploding behind her eyes. Hot colors and cold colors alternately controlled her, growing brighter and stronger and more frighteningly beautiful with every twist of the kaleidoscope.

"Miles," she cried, lost. He was stroking the rainbow to an arch so steep, so magnificent that she thought she could not stand to look at it.

"Miles," she called again as she reached the rainbow's crest, groping out to wind her fingers through his hair, as though he might keep her from falling.

But nothing could have stopped it. The rainbow shattered, breaking into a million glorious colors, a million glittering pieces, and she fell helplessly through them into a bottomless, roaring blackness.

He must have caught her, because when she breathed again she was in his arms, her head cradled against his chest. Her cheek felt damp, and her hair stuck to her shoulders. She reached up blindly, and her fingers found his jaw, his ear, the back of his neck. And she knew, as soon as she was capable of knowing anything again, that she would love him forever.

IT WAS ALMOST midnight before George showed up. Darcy had even allowed herself to hope he wouldn't come at all. Perhaps, she thought, the fates would let her have this one perfect evening.

She and Miles had arrived at the party flushed and late. They had danced every dance together, and the guests had just smiled knowingly, making gentle jests about the "lovebirds."

Once they had even slipped out onto the deck, where the music was muffled and not nearly as potent as the wind soughing in the palms. For a long, solitary interlude they stood entwined, looking toward the pool, which was lit from within. It glowed like a cask of liquid sapphires under the black sky.

Their bodies were comfortable together. Her head nestled against the hollow of his shoulder, and his arms wrapped easily around her waist, catching her just below her heart, which thrummed slowly against his hand. But they didn't speak. It was as though the intimacy their bodies had achieved had not yet spread to their voices, their minds. The peace was too fragile—a wrong word, a misjudged tone, might shatter it.

At some point Tessa stuck her head out through the open sliding glass doors. "Oops, sorry," she said, grinning, and ducked away again, pulling the door shut behind her. Miles chuckled, and tightened his hold. Though they both knew their roles as hosts required them to return, still they lingered in the moonlight.

It had been a little slice of heaven. And when they returned to the party and the hours wore on without any sign of George, she began to believe it might even last. The hurricane was headed toward the Gulf after all, the forecasters were reporting somberly, and several of tonight's guests had sent their regrets, saying they had decided to move inland for a few days. That might frighten George. He wasn't, in spite of his blustering, a particularly brave man.

Perhaps she and Miles would just go to bed early, and perhaps he would again work his miracles on her....

But just before the witching hour, when other, more civilized guests were checking their watches and thinking of home, George appeared in the doorway.

They'd been dancing. Her feet stumbled over the simple rhythm of the song, and Miles caught her with a strong hand in the small of her back.

"He's here."

Miles pressed her closer. "It's all right," he said in low tones. "He can't hurt you anymore."

But George had spotted them and was already making his way across the room. He didn't look drunk, she noted with relief. His face didn't have that puffy, red look she had come to dread. Several of the women nearby even smiled curiously, attracted by his burly, blond good looks.

"Darcy!" His voice was jocular. "You naughty girl. Sneaking off to get married. Why didn't you tell me?"

He leaned in toward her, obviously planning to envelop her in an avuncular hug, but Miles's arm tightened around her waist, and he edged her away deftly.

"Hello, George," Miles said smoothly. "Sorry we didn't send you a wedding invitation, but I guess we just got a little carried away. It was good of you to come all this way to wish us well."

She saw George's eyes narrow, and she realized that Miles had not been exaggerating the intensity of their enmity. George hated Miles every bit as much as Miles hated him.

But controlling his temper, George managed a smile. "Oh, I do, I do," he said heartily. "And I certainly congratulate you, Miles. You've landed quite a catch."

"Thank you." Miles pulled Darcy even closer. "I think so. Can we get you a drink?"

"No, thanks. I really just wanted to talk to Darcy a minute, if you can stand letting her out of your sight that long." He turned his smile on Darcy. "We've got a lot of little details to work out now, you know. Can you spare a few minutes?"

She nodded. This was inevitable. Better to get it over with now, when she was still filled with the sustaining warmth of Miles's lovemaking. "I'm sure Miles won't mind," she said calmly, "if we use the library. Will you, Miles?"

Miles's face was stiff. "I'll come with you."

She shook her head. "That's not necessary, really. You stay out here with your friends. It'll only take a minute."

He frowned. "Are you sure?"

Smiling, she nodded. "Sure."

His arm dropped from around her waist, and immediately she felt the loss of its support. But she kept her chin up and moved toward the library. "This way, then," she said, motioning to George.

He followed a few steps and then stopped, turning back toward Miles. "Oh, by the way," he said, his voice ostentatiously casual. Her heart pinched. She knew that tone. It always meant mischief.

"Yes?" Miles's brows went up.

"I was just wondering..." George grinned. "How's Connie?"

A surprising silence followed the question. Darcy looked in confusion from one to the other. George's smile grew even wider, but Miles's face might have been carved from stone. Slowly a dark flush appeared on each high cheekbone.

"She's fine," he said through teeth that might have been clenched. "Just fine."

"Oh, good," George said, turning away, his blue eyes alight with malicious pleasure. "Connie's a great gal, isn't she?"

Miles didn't answer, and George didn't seem to expect him to. He chuckled softly as he followed Darcy into the library.

When she closed the door behind them, she stood stiffly with her back against it.

"What do you want, George? Why did you come here?"

The smiling facade had fallen from him like an old set of clothes. "Did you think I wouldn't?" He went to the liquor cabinet and, as if the house belonged to him, poured himself a liberal tumbler of whiskey. "I've been to see Stone, too, and told him he'd better look this one over pretty carefully. Ever heard of collusion?"

She made a quick sound of disgust, and he tossed back the drink in one gulp.

"Oh, yes, honey, I know what's going on here. Did you think I wouldn't know what a farce this whole thing is? That snuggling lovebirds act out there was just too pathetic. You and Miles Hawthorne? What a joke! This is a marriage made in Wall Street, baby, not in heaven."

"You're wrong, George," she said softly, remembering the feel of Miles's lips on her skin. She flushed at the memory. "I know you're angry, but, really, you're wrong."

"Oh, no, I'm not. And if he's persuaded you he's in love with you then you're a fool. You want to know why he married you? He and I go back a long way. Why I remember one night at the club—"

"I know all about that." She drew herself up, trying not to reveal how his words stung. This was so like George, coming in to poison any happiness she might have found. "He told me."

"And you still think this is a love match? Grow up, baby," he said, dropping the tumbler back on the silver tray. "Why don't you ask him who Connie is? Or do you already know that, too?"

Her stomach twisted, and she bit her lower lip against the pain. "Why don't *you* tell me, George," she said scornfully, "if you think it's so important?"

He laughed, a mean, mirthless sound. "Nope. I think you should hear this little gem from your darling husband. He's the one who signs her rent checks, after all."

With a one-sided smirk he watched the heat rise to her cheeks. She didn't know what to say—her courage had suddenly left her, like a sail that has been turned away from the wind that filled it.

He chuckled again. "This isn't going to be as easy as you thought, is it? I've still got the shares your mother left to me, and I think I can manage to keep control of Tessa's shares, too. This marriage has to meet with Stone's approval before you take over the business, and somehow I just don't think it's going to."

He poured another drink and stuffed the glass into her passive hand. "Here, baby. Try this. You look like you could use a drink. And don't worry. I'll just let myself out."

JUST AS GEORGE HAD intended, from that moment the party was spoiled for her. Miles stood beside her, but the glow was gone. All she could feel was the gnaw of jealousy, the scratch of distrust and the isolation of knowing that she wasn't close enough to her own husband to ask him the question that pressed against her heart: Who is Connie to you?

And so she drank too much. The wine flowed freely. Half a dozen couples stayed on and on, dancing and drinking, and she drank with them, hoping to dull the ache that George had given her.

It helped a little—until Alice, bedecked in black and white lace, came in looking disturbed and whispered something in Miles's ear. Darcy caught only one word. Connie. Miles frowned sharply and, excusing himself with a quick squeeze of Darcy's shoulders, followed the maid through the hall into the kitchen.

Connie...

And then the drinks worked against her. Evan asked her to dance and kept up a constant patter of small talk, about the coming hurricane, about the party, about Emily... She could hardly hear him. Over and over, in her mind, the question thundered: Who is Connie?

"Who is Connie?"

Evan pulled back, looking shocked. He had been mid-sentence, probably rhapsodizing about Emily, and the question obviously caught him unprepared.

"Connie who?" But an elusive quality shadowed his face, and it wasn't like him.

The drinks had made her stubborn. "Connie," she said flatly, refusing to believe he didn't know. "Connie, the pretty blonde with the little boy."

"Oh," he said slowly. "Yeah. Connie is an old friend of ours. Her family and our family... all that stuff, for years. She lives here on the island. She works at the boat yard. Secretary, you know, and kind of a receptionist."

She tried to look arch, hoping he wouldn't realize her questions were anything but curiosity. *"Old friend?"* she teased. "Come on, Evan, it was more than that for Miles, wasn't it?"

Evan looked embarrassed. "Well, a long time ago, maybe. It was ages ago, really. Years ago. At least."

"And..." she prompted.

"And, well, they were going to get married. But they didn't. And it was so long ago. Now they're just friends, really. She's been in kind of a bad spot for the past few years, and he's been helping her out, gave her the job and all. We've known her since we were kids." He smiled, pride wrinkling his eyes. "That's the kind of guy Miles is. He never deserts a friend."

"Why doesn't her husband help her?"

And finally Evan did look uncomfortable, as though she had said the one thing he had been dreading. "I don't know," he said, his glance darting around the room. "I really don't know very much about it. I just know she's been in a bind and Miles has been helping out. That's all I know."

But his eyes, his sweet, troubled brown eyes, told her all she needed to know. There was no husband. There never had been. There was only Miles, who would never desert a friend in trouble. Only Miles, who carried the little boy so proudly on his shoulders. Only Miles, who had left her side to answer a whispered summons....

She hadn't quite realized how drunk she was until she began to cry. She dropped her head to Evan's shoulder and shook silently, tears rolling onto his jacket.

"Darcy, what—" He tried to grab her shoulders and pull her erect, but she was too limp a burden. He looked around frantically for a moment, and then, holding her up against him, danced toward the sliding glass doors. A quick pull, and they were out of the bright lights and into the dusky darkness. Out of the air-conditioning and into the windless humidity. And still her tears flowed, as though they rose from a bottomless fountain.

"Darcy, what on earth is the matter? It's not Connie, is it?" His voice was almost squeaking with dismay. "Believe me, that's been over forever. It's nothing for you to be upset about."

She shook her head, too far gone in drink and misery to care what he thought of her. "No, it's not that," she said, choking. "It's just—everything. Oh, Evan." She put her head back on his shoulder and wept harder.

"Evan, it was such a mistake. The whole marriage was such a mistake. Nothing has ever hurt so much. Nothing."

"Why?" His voice was breathless, aghast. "Is Miles unkind to you?"

"Yes," she sobbed. "No. Oh, I don't know. It isn't his fault." How could it be Miles's fault? He hadn't asked her to love him. He hadn't ever promised to love her. It should have been such a clean, simple business deal, and somehow she had let it get out of control. "It's all my fault," she said.

"No, Darcy, of course it's not," he said, patting her shoulder, clearly unable to imagine what she was talking about. "Maybe you should just go to bed, and things will look better in the morning. It was a strain seeing George tonight, and you must be very tired."

She hiccuped slightly. "Yes," she said, struggling to compose herself. "It *was* a mistake. The whole thing, the whole marriage was a mistake..."

She couldn't find the composure she sought. "I think I'd better go upstairs."

"Sure." He offered her his arm. They turned toward the sliding glass doors and both stopped, comically frozen in their tracks, when they saw Miles standing there.

Even Evan felt Miles's displeasure this time. "I was just going to take Darcy upstairs," he began and flushed at the choice of words. "I mean, she's not feeling well, and—"

"You mean she's had too much to drink." Miles's voice was flat and hard.

Evan's shoulders stiffened at the tone. "I mean she's not feeling well, Miles. She wants to go upstairs."

"Then I'll take her," Miles said stonily, holding out his hand. "I am her husband, after all."

Evan didn't relinquish her arm, and Darcy felt him go steely and tough. Absently she registered that this was a new side of Evan. It must be a strength that Emily had brought out in him.

"Well, if you were a very good husband, she wouldn't be crying like this, would she?"

Miles's face was like a hurricane itself—black emotions whirling across his features with storm force. His eyes narrowed to dark slits. "Am I to understand that you think you could have done better?"

"Damn it, I *know* I could have," Evan shot back.

Darcy wrenched her arm away. She'd heard enough. "Stop it, both of you," she cried. "This is the most ridiculous conversation I've ever heard. I can find my own way upstairs, thank you. I've had too much to drink, Miles, that's true. But I'm not so drunk I can't find my own bedroom door."

He stood back, as stiff as a robot, to let her pass. "I take it this means you'd rather I didn't join you?"

"Maybe I'd better be alone tonight," she said, the stupid tears ready to overtake her again. She groped for a balancing spot along the door frame. "I'm really not . . . feeling well."

"As you like," he said, his voice reflecting only utter indifference. "I'll say good-night to everyone for you."

And even though her arm brushed his chest as she passed, he didn't move a muscle. He might have been a tall, bronze statue. He couldn't have been the same man who, just hours ago, had taken her riding on a rainbow. . . .

With misery nipping at her heels, she fled.

CHAPTER NINE

THE NEXT MORNING dawned yellow and hazy, and she could tell by the strange, wet stillness in the air that the hurricane was coming. It didn't matter to her. Her head pounded, and her stomach waffled, like a boat on rocky waters. She put her aching head under the satin pillow and tried to go back to sleep.

But too much commotion assailed her sensitive ears. The sounds of doors slamming, voices calling, cars starting, hammers pounding. Gradually, though her mind was still numb, she pieced it together. They were boarding up Two Palms. The hurricane was coming, all right. It must be coming soon.

And still she didn't care. After what she had been through last night, what could a hurricane do?

Connie was the force that would destroy her happiness—not a storm, just one woman. Connie, who had been Miles's love long before Darcy had ever met him. Connie, whose rent checks were signed with Miles Hawthorne's strong hand, and whose son rode his shoulders with the perfect aplomb of one who belonged there.

Oh, why had she taken so long to face it? The little boy must be Miles's son. He must be. She squeezed the pillow against her eyes, trying to block out the weird yellow light and the traumatic fact. But neither one of them would go away.

She groped to remember every inch of the boy's face. Where was the haunting familiarity—in what feature did the revealing resemblance hide? Feature by feature she dissected it but found nothing definite. It would be unfair to say he actually *looked* like Miles. He looked just like his mother, really. But there was something...something small that lingered in his blue eyes like the ghost of a memory.

Frustrated, she flung the pillow aside and stood up. As much as she would like to, she couldn't cower in bed all day. All too true to his word, Miles had not come to her last night. Though she'd lain awake waiting, she hadn't even heard him come upstairs at all.

Her heart skidded, and she shoved the horrible thought aside violently. No! He couldn't have. He couldn't have spent the night anywhere else—not after what they had shared together.

She met her shadowed eyes in the mirror and saw the question they asked. What *had* they shared? For her, it had been cataclysmic, a surrender of body and soul that was total and permanent. For him—how could she tell? He was clearly an accomplished lover. Perhaps every woman he touched felt transformed, abdicated. He had never spoken the word of love.

The hammering grew louder, and she pulled on a pair of cut-off bluejeans and a T-shirt. Perhaps a cup of coffee might still the hammering *inside* her head. It was time to face the storm.

She barely missed colliding with one of the maids, who scurried past her unseeing, as Darcy headed for Tessa's door. She rapped lightly.

"Come in—oh, Darcy, thank goodness you're up! Miles said we mustn't wake you, but you just kept sleeping and sleeping, and I was getting worried. The hurricane has turned north or west or something, any-how they think we're going to get it by tonight.''

"Northwest," Darcy corrected automatically. She finally noticed the suitcase Tessa had half filled on the bed. "Is it that bad? Is it really going to hit Sanibel Island?''

"I don't know," Tessa said. "I just know Miles says we have to leave the island. He says we have to do it soon, before the rain starts. He says the causeway can get really backed up with everybody trying to evacuate at once.''

Tessa went to the window and peered out. "It doesn't look much like a hurricane, does it? It's so still. But Miles says in a couple of hours it'll turn black and windy and really nasty. It sounds exciting." Her voice was wistful. "I've never seen a hurricane. I wish I could stay.''

"Don't be silly," Darcy said sternly. "If Miles thinks we should evacuate, he must have a good reason.''

Pouting, Tessa turned back to the suitcase. "Well, if it's so dangerous, how come *he's* staying?''

Darcy stared. "Is he?''

"Yeah." Tessa tossed a pair of sneakers on top of the clothes. "Is that fair?''

Darcy's cheeks felt cold, as though the predicted wind had already blown across them. "Where is he now?" she asked, ignoring Tessa's question.

"Over at the marina, I think. There's some kind of problem.''

Darcy swiveled and moved out of the room and down the hall quickly, her sneakers soundless on the carpet. Tessa's voice was fading out behind her.

"Darcy, where are you going? Miles said you had to pack as soon as you got up....''

She didn't stop to answer. Her head still pounding, she left the house and climbed into the little rental car, revving the motor angrily. So he was sending them away, was he? Well, if he wanted to get rid of her, he'd have to come right out and tell her so. She wouldn't let him hide behind this chivalrous facade.

The marina was alive with life, the hurricane bringing more people out than any sunny summer day. Men strode back and forth, grim-faced, barking orders to tanned teens in white shorts who jogged obediently from one boat to another.

The wind had already picked up. Sails snapped as the young men fought to lower them. The air held an ominous drumbeat beneath the falsetto cry of seabirds circling dizzily overhead. The hazy light had grown dingy, more gray than yellow, and the air had a wet, salty flavor.

She stood near the bait shop, ignoring the rancid, fishy smell, and wondered how she'd ever find Miles in this crowd. She didn't even know which boat was his.

"What are you doing here? Have you packed?"

She whirled at the deep, brusque sound. Miles stood at the door of the bait shop, his white knit shirt ruffling in the accelerating wind, his dark hair feathering around his unsmiling face.

He looked angry, or worried, or both. His dark brows were a straight line, with a deep furrow between them. Dark shadows lay like smudges under his eyes. Her own indignation faltered, in the face of what was obviously a genuine crisis, and she felt ridiculous to have come storming over here to confront him. All these other people were equally rushed, equally concerned. The hurricane was *real,* not just some convenient excuse he had invented to get rid of her.

"Not yet," she said, uncomfortably. She licked her lips and tasted salt. "I just wanted to ask you what's going on. Is the hurricane coming here? Tessa doesn't seem to know." She tried to smile. "Coordinates bore her."

He didn't return the smile. "They think it's going to come in a good bit north of here, maybe as far north as Tampa," he said in clipped tones. "But we're going to feel it. It could be ugly."

"She said we had to evacuate. Surely that's an exaggeration? If it's not coming in at Sanibel—"

"It's no exaggeration. We'll still get a lot of rain, a lot of wind. And the island is so unprotected." He looked around him wearily. "Any boats left here tonight could be driftwood by tomorrow morning. There could be floods. We could lose power. And if there is a storm surge..." He shut his eyes briefly, as though unable to pursue that thought.

"Anyhow, you definitely do need to evacuate," he went on. "Evan is ready to drive you and Tessa off the island as soon as you're packed. We're not the only ones with that idea, either, so go get packed before the causeway is a parking lot."

"But, Miles..." She didn't know what to say. She just didn't want to leave without him. "Maybe it won't be that bad. Maybe I could stay—"

"No, dammit." He took her roughly by the shoulders and turned her toward the water, where tiny foamy crowns had begun to form on the jagged water. "See those whitecaps? Pretty soon the wind will slice them right off the waves and fling them through the air. Later the wind will be so bad the rain will drive sideways, and grains of sand will blast everything. It'll take the paint off your car. If you're out here, it will draw blood."

He whipped her around. "You think I'd let you stay?" He let go of her shoulders abruptly, shoving her toward the small adjacent parking lot. "Go. Get packed and get out of here."

She stumbled but found her balance. "What about you, Miles? I want you to come, too. If it is dangerous for me, then it's just as dangerous for you."

"No, it's not. I know how to handle hurricanes. It isn't my first."

She clenched her fists, anxiety making her angry. "No one can *handle* a hurricane. Come with me."

He rubbed his face hard and ran his hands through his tousled hair. Rain had begun to fall in tiny, sharp needles. "I can't."

"Why not?" Her voice, which had risen to be heard above the low moan of the wind, was akin to a cry. "Why not?"

A dull misery smothered his features. "It's Trevor."

"Who's Trevor?" But she knew. With a drowning sense of misery, she knew.

"He's the son of a friend of mine. He's only five. He ran away a couple of hours ago. I can't go anywhere until we've found him."

Even as he spoke, his gaze darted around the marina, as though he might find him there. The pain in his eyes was like a fire, and she drew back, feeling burned by its heat.

"Connie's little boy?" She didn't know if he would hear the words. He didn't seem to be listening. His eyes were still roaming, probing, as though by force of will he could make the little boy materialize.

But she waited, needing an answer. And as she stood, numbed with the stinging rain and the overwhelming sense of misery, unable to move or speak, she got her answer. Connie, her clothes soggy and her blond hair stuck in darkened spikes to her cheeks, ran up to Miles and pressed her hands against his chest in a gesture of desperate imploring.

Miles looked down at her, his eyes dark and, pressing his own strong hands over hers, murmured something Darcy couldn't hear. Then they started to walk quickly away, Miles's arm around Connie's shaking shoulders. He apparently had forgotten Darcy's presence.

He was halfway down the dock when he turned and called back, over the wind. "Go home, Darcy. Get packed and get off this island."

NO ONE in the little car spoke at all. Tessa was still pouting. She thought the storm was exhilarating and didn't want to have to leave. She had once heard that some people held hurricane parties, and she wanted to have one, too. Miles was mean, she declared.

Evan needed all his concentration to maneuver the congested streets. Who would have imagined that tiny Sanibel Island could hold so many people? If only there had been some real warning! But Hurricane Jean had not been thoughtful. She'd hovered for days at the tip of Florida, teasingly considering both the Gulf and the Atlantic, and then at the last minute had decided on the Gulf, whirling up the western coast of the state.

So now hundreds of cars crawled along the narrow streets. The wind was high. The Australian pines that lined Periwinkle Way tossed their heads furiously and threw pine needles down by the fistful, clogging the wipers. The rain was so heavy it was as thick as milk on the windshield, and only the watery red glow of twin taillights ahead showed Evan where the street was.

Darcy didn't speak because she was drowning in her own miserable thoughts. She'd tried to be angry. She had tossed clothes into her suitcase viciously, punctuating each new toss with a furious question. Why should Miles take this risk? Why should he stay on this vulnerable little island, waiting for the winds to blow the roof from over his head, or for the waters to surge in and carry him away? Why didn't he come with them, with his wife?

But even at her most tearful, she had known he was doing the right thing. Even if the child were *not* his son, Miles was the kind of man who would stay and help. For just a moment, Connie's pain flashed through her mind, and the intensity of it blinded her. To think of that sweet-faced, blond little boy huddling somewhere, frightened by the howling wind, the driving rain, lost....

"No!" she cried, and Evan jumped, startled by the sudden noise.

"What? What's wrong?"

"I have to go back." She leaned over and tugged on his sleeve. "Take me back to Two Palms."

"Are you crazy?" He returned his attention to the swarming street. "We're lucky to be getting out of here. We're not going back."

"I am." Her voice held an implacable determination. "I'm going if I have to walk back."

"Darcy, don't." Tessa was almost whining. "Miles said we had to leave."

"I'm going back." She put her hand on the door handle meaningfully. "Am I walking?"

Evan threw her a bewildered look but, obviously correctly interpreting the expression on her face, flipped on his blinker. "Of course you're not walking. God knows how I'm going to explain this to Miles, but I wouldn't even *try* to explain it if you walked back."

The streets were clear in that direction—no one in his right mind, Evan muttered, was going *back* to the island. In only a few minutes they pulled into the driveway at Two Palms.

She wrenched the door open, squinting against the blast of rain. "Thanks, Evan," she said. "Now hurry. You and Tessa get going. I'll get Miles to bring me to the mainland when we find Trevor."

Without waiting for his answer—what was the use of arguing in this rain?—she slammed the car door and raced toward the house. As soon as she reached the porch, where she stood dripping and watching Evan's little car crunch across the coquina drive, its tires spraying water like a spinning sparkler, she began to wonder whether she was as crazy as Evan had suggested.

For one thing, how was she going to find Miles again? He could be anywhere. And for another, what right did she have to be here? If Trevor *was* Miles's son, then this was a crisis he would want to meet with Connie, and Connie alone.

She couldn't answer those questions. But somehow it didn't matter. All that mattered was that a little boy was lost and afraid, and that Miles was hurting. She loved Miles—she had faced that last night. Perhaps that was foolish, even dangerous, but it was true. And she had to be with him now, to face whatever might happen.

The door had opened behind her, and Miles stood on the threshold, his arms spread high against the doorframe. His shirt was soaked, clinging to his body, and his hair glistened with moisture.

"Where's Evan? Dammit—I told him to make sure you—" Again the angry words, only this time they were more than angry. They were furious.

"Don't blame Evan," she said, putting her hands against his cold chest. The shirt was like a second skin on him, and she could feel his muscles distinctly beneath it. "He didn't have any choice. I made him bring me back. Miles, I—" She faltered under his grim, unyielding gaze. "I want to help."

His dark eyes didn't soften. "You can't. It's too dangerous. A couple of power lines are already down over on Captiva. You could get killed."

"I won't." The rain drove at a slant, attacking them on the porch, and he pulled her into the house, slamming the door behind them. "I'll be careful," she finished, her voice sounding unnaturally loud in the strange quiet of the house. "I'll be okay."

The strident trill of the telephone sounded from the greatroom, and releasing her abruptly, he moved to answer it.

After a few monosyllabic responses, he dropped the receiver and turned to her. She thought his face might have lightened, if only by a fraction of a degree.

"Some people think they saw a little boy down at Hibiscus Plaza. I've got to go."

She opened the door, ignoring the rain that pelted her. "I'm going with you."

His face darkened again, and she cut in briskly, before he could object. "The plaza is a big place. If I'm there we can each take a side and it will go much faster." She gave him her most level look. "Don't waste time trying to talk me out of it, Miles. I'm going."

He joined her at the door, and under the tension she thought she could see the ghost of a smile. "Guns and beer bottles, and now this.'' He touched her cheek with a wet, cool hand. "You're a very determined woman, aren't you?"

She nodded, heat rising through her in spite of her sodden clothes, her dripping hair. His touch was like a fire that could burn away the rain.

But he took his hand away, as though he hadn't even noticed her reaction, and ran it through his hair again. "Hurry, then," he said roughly, bending his head to meet the rain. "I'll never forgive myself if I don't find him."

THE QUAINT open wooden shopping center was strangely deserted. No one was thinking of swimsuits, conch shells, souvenir T-shirts and jewelry today. Anyone who was left on the island was probably over at Bailey's General Store, scooping up all the batteries, Sterno, bottled water and canned goods they could carry.

Miles parked the car in the middle of the empty lot, and they ran out in opposite directions toward the dark and glistening stores. Darcy took the right, the side of the mall with the shell store, and began calling.

"Trevor!" Her voice was whipped away by the wind, and she tried again, putting more breath behind it. "Trevor!"

The wind carried a hollow echo of Miles's voice to her, too. "Trevor!" he called from the other side of the long open plaza. "Trevor, it's Miles."

She rattled doorknobs, peered in through the cracks in boarded windows and, always, always, kept calling.

The wooden boardwalk was slippery, and she lost her footing often as she ran. When the wind gusted, she held on to one of the pillars that supported the roof and waited for it to pass. When she finished with the front, she raced around back. The ground was mushy underfoot, and mud sprayed up around her ankles.

She even looked in the dumpsters behind the stores. She got down on her hands and knees and checked for a crawl space. There wasn't one.

Finally, muddy and heartsick, she headed back to the car. Miles was there, too, his face an expressionless mask under the rivulets of rain that criss-crossed it.

"We'd better get back to the house," he said. "Someone else might call."

The return drive was slower. She strained her eyes trying to see through the speckled window, hoping for the sight of a wet blond head.

She didn't look at Miles, felt unable to endure the misery she would see there. He'd never forgive himself, he had said.

"It isn't your fault," she said impulsively, the words falling into the emptiness of the car, and then regretted it. What did she know about this horrible situation? Nothing. And yet somehow she knew it *couldn't* be Miles's fault.

He didn't answer, but she felt the tension tighten in him.

"It isn't," she repeated. "You mustn't blame yourself."

"Oh, yes it is, damn it," he said suddenly, explosively, looking over at her with a palpable fury. "It *is* my fault. I should have seen it coming. I should have known George would do something like this. I should have known it the minute I married you. He's a dangerous bastard, and I should have done something to protect Trevor."

She shrank against the side of the car, horrified. "George?" Her voice was a thin reed. "George had something to do with this?"

"You're damn right he did." Miles swung the car sharply around a curve, sending a virtual tidal wave arcing from the tires. "What a fool I was not to see it coming!" Absently, he swiped a hand across his forehead. "It might never have happened if I hadn't married you."

After that they didn't speak. What was left to say? As the car pulled into Two Palms, she checked the car clock. Only five—she'd thought it was much later. It was as pitch black as any moonless midnight.

They darted through the rain toward the house, and he went straight for the telephone. More cryptic monosyllables, giving no sign of hope or despair, and then he turned again to her.

This time his face was desperately earnest, and he put his hands on her shoulders.

"You have to stay here. Will you do that for me, Darcy? Will you stay here?"

"Why?" Her voice was a whisper, but she knew already that she would do whatever he asked. If George had hurt Trevor, if her marriage had somehow brought this pain to Miles...she didn't know how she would bear it. And she knew, with a black, crashing pain, that her marriage would never survive it.

"I have to go to the marina again," Miles was saying. "This makes twice now he—or some kid—has been reported around my boat. I was looking for him there earlier, when you came. But he wasn't there then, and he might not be there now. It's the most dangerous spot on the island, and he's got too much sense to stay at the marina in this weather. I hope."

Her heart squeezed so hard she winced. She knew he had to go, and yet she was so afraid. She didn't argue, but her eyes were full and they begged silently.

"I can't let you come," he said. "And besides, someone should be here, in case he comes here." His hands tightened at his sides. "Don't fight me on this. Stay here."

And then he was gone.

THE LIGHTS went out just before seven o'clock. She lit candles around the greatroom, noticing with pride that her hand shook only a little as she held the matches. But the candles didn't help much, offering pitiful little circles of strange orange light in the huge blackness of the room. Everything smelled ominously of salt water and sulphur, and, as though set free from their usual restraints, shadows cavorted on the walls and ceiling.

She sat as if frozen in the armchair and tried not to think. The crackle of the radio, tuned to the weather band, continued, and occasionally she caught a sentence or two. It sounded as though Sanibel might be spared the worst of the storm. That was good. She tried to believe it was good enough.

But winds were reported at sixty-five miles an hour, not officially hurricane strength but plenty strong enough to blow a mast off a sailboat and send it through the air like a weapon. Strong enough to knock a man off his feet—a man or a little boy.

Her fingers clutched the arms of the chair as the rain dashed itself against the awnings, which had been so carefully screwed shut. And everywhere was the high whine of the wind. She shut her eyes, to shut out the shadows that danced and laughed. Two hours. He had been gone for two hours. Surely that was too long.

The new sound was so tiny she almost didn't hear it. A kitten, perhaps? A mewing, a lost, frightened mewing? And then a rapping? Her eyes flew open and she listened, trying to separate the sounds. That was the rain. That was the house, creaking and objecting to the winds that assaulted it. That was the surf. And that . . . that was knocking.

Bolting out of her chair, she flung open the door.

"Miles," the little boy said, his tiny voice pathetic in the keening winds. "I have to find Miles."

CHAPTER TEN

WITHOUT THINKING, without wondering whether he would want her to, she scooped Trevor up in her arms, holding his wet, shivering body against the warmth of her own.

"Oh, honey," she murmured, kicking the door shut with her foot and carrying him to the sofa. "Honey, we're so glad to see you. We've been so worried about you."

He lifted his face from her shoulder and looked around the room, his blue eyes wet from tears and rain. "Where's Miles?"

Dropping to the sofa without relaxing her hold on him, she rocked him gently. She ran her hands across his back, trying to rub some warmth into his thin little body.

She was crying, too, tears of relief streaming unchecked down her cheeks. "He went out to look for *you,*" she said, forcing bravado into her voice. After all Trevor had been through, she mustn't alarm him. "He'll be back soon, and he'll be so happy that you're here."

He shivered again, and she grabbed the afghan from the back of the couch and swaddled him in it, still rocking, still rubbing. *Oh, Miles,* she said silently, willing the message across the storm, *come home. Come home*.

"My mother..." The voice was little again, the blue eyes anxious, peering out through the fuzzy colors of the afghan.

Guilt washed over her like a dousing of hot water. How could she have forgotten Connie? How could she have let the frantic mother spend even one extra minute in torment?

"She's probably at home, honey, waiting for you." She eased him down onto the sofa, tucking the afghan around his shoulders. "I'd better call her and tell her you're okay." Impulsively, she kissed his wet hair. "Oh, Trevor, thank God you're all right."

"Mother will be mad, but I—" He clutched the afghan in two small fists and pulled it tighter around his neck.

"No, she won't," she protested quickly. "She's going to be very happy." With one last kiss, she headed for the telephone, praying that the lines were still working. The solid hum reassured her, and she leaned against the wall, her knees weak with relief. "Do you know your phone number?"

He did, like a well-trained young man, and he told her slowly and carefully. But the infuriating beep-beep of a busy signal was the only response. Connie was on the phone....

"We'll try again in a minute," she said, cradling the receiver. "She's probably talking to—"

The door flung open, and more driving rain puddled on the floorboards as Miles came inside slowly, his dark, soaking form wearing an air of dejection. Without speaking, he closed the door.

"Miles! Oh, Miles, you're all right," she said incoherently, relief fighting with her eagerness to tell the good news. "Trevor came here—"

But he probably never heard her. The small lump under the afghan moved, stared, gave a joyous cry, and then catapulted across the room.

"Miles! You're back!" Trevor flung himself into the older man like a tackle. "I've been waiting for you forever."'

Miles's face wore a look of stunned disbelief, as though he had been so far removed from hope that he couldn't accept even the proof before his eyes.

"Trevor!" The child wrapped his arms around Miles's legs and clung. With a deep, incredulous, meaningless groan, Miles squatted down to embrace the little boy. His voice was husky. "*You've* been waiting for *me?*" He smiled and chucked Trevor under the chin. "Hey, you gave us quite a scare, partner."

"I'm s-sorry." Trevor did look sorry, bedraggled and ashamed. "I really am."

Holding the child closely, Miles looked up at Darcy. "Did you call Connie?"

"I tried," she said, her hand still on the telephone. They were both safe, the man she loved and the boy he loved. Relief was pouring through her. So why did she feel so lost? Why did she feel so empty? "The line was busy."

He stood up. "I'll try." Turning to Trevor, he said firmly, "You need a warm bath, young man, before you catch pneumonia." He gave Darcy a questioning look. "Would you mind?"

"Of course not." She let go of the telephone. It was natural, of course, that Miles would want to be the one to tell Connie. She smiled at Trevor. "They filled the bathtubs earlier, in case the water went out. All we have to do is add some warm water, and it'll be all ready for you."

She picked up one of the candles, its flame dancing across his face. "I'll bet you've never had a bath by candlelight before, have you? It'll be fun."

Trevor looked dubious. Like all little boys, he probably couldn't imagine any kind of bath being fun. But he sloshed along obediently behind her.

As she climbed the stairs, she heard Miles's deep voice, still husky, still edged with a thrill of awe at the miracle that had come to them. "Connie. Connie, he's all right. He's come home, safe and sound."

And then she shut her ears so that she couldn't hear any more.

HALF AN HOUR later, when the doorbell rang, Trevor was ready. He wore one of Tessa's T-shirts, which grazed his ankles, and his hair was almost blond again, toweled dry and neatly brushed. He sat soberly on the sofa, drinking a cup of tepid chocolate and listening to Miles, who was trying to explain how worried everyone had been.

"That's Mommy now," Miles said, giving Trevor an encouraging smile. "And remember, if she's upset, it's just because she's been so frightened for you."

But Connie was joyful. Darcy stood in the shadows, clutching her own cup of chocolate and watched as Connie held out her arms to her son. "Darling!" she cried. "Thank God."

An incoherent cry burst from her as Trevor ran into her arms. With a strange mixture of weeping and laughing, she embraced her son as though, if she held him close enough, she would never lose him again. Trevor began to cry, too, finally abandoning his brave-little-soldier act now that his mother was there to protect him.

After a long moment, Connie held out her arms to Miles, too. Darcy's breath froze as he moved easily into them.

"How can I thank you, Miles?" Connie's voice broke as she rested her head against his strong shoulder. "How can I *ever* thank you?"

"Shhh," he murmured, stroking her back. "Everything is okay now."

They stood that way, arms entwined, for what seemed like forever. The candlelight threw huge, exaggerated silhouettes onto the wall, and the intimacy of their circle excluded Darcy so completely she might have been in another world.

And yet she must not have been, because when the cup fell from her hand they heard her. It clattered onto the cushioned flooring and rolled away under the cabinet, leaving a thin brown trail of chocolate.

"Darcy!" Miles disengaged himself and held out his hand. "Come see Connie."

She had squatted down to pick up the cup, but at his command she felt herself rising. She smoothed her muddy hair out of her eyes. There had been no time to bathe or even to brush her own hair, so she knew she must look a mess. But that didn't matter, did it? Jealousy and petty vanity had no place in a moment of this magnitude.

"Hi," she said, moving out of the shadows and giving her best smile. "I'm so glad Trevor is safe."

"Darcy is the one who found him, Connie. I had sent her off with Evan, but she came back. She came back to help."

Connie stepped forward slowly and put out her hand. "Thank you, Darcy. I'll always be grateful."

With an extreme effort Darcy took the extended hand. "I didn't do anything but wait," she said, shaking her head. "Miles took all the risks."

The smile Connie turned on Miles was dazzling. "Yes, he's quite wonderful, isn't he?"

Dumbly Darcy nodded and let her hand fall. Yes, he was wonderful. She looked over at him, dirty and wet and obviously tired but still the most devastatingly handsome man she had ever seen. Still the man she loved.

Connie scooped Trevor up into her arms and squeezed him. She looked at Darcy. "Would you like to come in the car with us? There's room for everybody. And there's still electricity at the hotel."

Darcy looked at Miles, her eyes speaking the question her lips were too numb to form.

He shook his head. "No, thanks. We've got things to do here." He nodded reassuringly at Connie, who was frowning at him over Trevor's head. "Don't worry about us. The last word I heard on the weather band was that the hurricane's coming in way up near Gainesville. It probably won't get any worse here on Sanibel than it is right now."

"Okay," she said, her worried frown giving way to a smile, too. "Thanks, then, for everything. And Darcy—"

Darcy looked up, surprised at the note of friendliness she heard.

"Darcy, I want to thank you for being so...so supportive. You didn't have to help tonight. You're a good person, and I'm—I'm glad you married Miles." She raised her brows and grinned sheepishly at Miles, absently patting Trevor on his sleepy head. "Well, I *am* glad. I know I've been a millstone around your neck, but I've grown up a lot lately, and I really am glad. I hope you'll be happy."

Darcy murmured thanks, unable to meet Miles's gaze. She knew, and of course he knew, that any happiness they found would be found separately, not as a couple. But it was generous of Connie to say so, more generous than *she* could have been in the same situation. She could never have reconciled herself to letting Miles go....

Amid a flurry of thanks and goodbyes, Miles opened a huge gold golf umbrella and walked the pair of them out to the waiting car. The rain's pounding cloaked their words, and Darcy was grateful for that. She didn't want to hear their private goodbyes. She stood staring at a dying candle.

When he came back in, he was very quiet. He closed the door, put the umbrella in its stand and then stood without speaking, his brown eyes black in the shadows.

She didn't know what to say. The windowless room was hot and close, as though the candle flames had burned away all the fresh air. Now the flames were so tired they no longer sent shadows dancing on the walls. They just sputtered low in their deep cradles of melted wax.

Even the wind sounded tired. It was only a low wuthering, as if nature's rage had given way to despair.

"Well, Darcy—what now?" His voice was almost harsh.

"I don't know." She didn't look at him. She dipped her finger in the hot wax, and it molded instantly to her fingertip. The faint burning was nothing compared to the bigger burning inside her heart.

"Do you want to go back to the mainland? I can take you, if you'd like."

As she watched, the flame sank beneath the scalding wax and died. "I don't know."

"Or you could stay here . . . with me." His voice was bland, indicating no preference one way or the other.

"No." She ground her teeth together, trying not to ask him any questions. She wouldn't beg him to explain things to her. She wouldn't. But she couldn't stop herself.

"Oh, Miles—Miles, I have to know." The words burst from her like air from a popped balloon. "I have to know about Connie."

He made a small sound of annoyance. "What about her?"

"Everything. The truth. Evan said you were engaged to her." Finally she dared to look up at him. It had been said, and she was, though fearful, strangely relieved, like the sick person who finally decides to let the doctor run his tests. She'd avoided the issue far too long. "And George told me you pay her rent."

"Ahhh." His eyes narrowed. "Good old George, always trying to sink someone else's boat." He tilted his head and gave her a steady look. "That's all technically true. We were engaged—once, a long time ago. And I have been helping her out, partly by paying her rent."

"And what about Trevor?" She was surprised at how calm she sounded. A hammer of fear was knocking at her breast.

"Trevor?" His hand dropped, and his lips whitened. The fire in his eyes was stark fury, nothing less. "What about him? What did that bastard George say about Trevor?"

"Who is his father?"

He cursed and turned away. Running his hands through his hair roughly, he spoke with his back to her. "I can't tell you. Connie asked me not to tell you about Trevor."

The knocking within her grew louder, more painful. It was as good as an admission. And then her heart burst. It simply exploded, in a melting, fiery mass of pain.

"Oh, God," she moaned as the pain spread out to her limbs. If she hadn't been against the wall, she might have fallen. "He is yours, then. He's your son."

"*My* son?" He whipped around, his whole body rigid. Coming toward her in a flash, he grabbed her, shaking her as though he could shake the idea right out of her mind. "Is *that* what you thought? You thought Trevor was my son?"

She nodded, dizzied by the shaking and the pain.

His eyes glittered, reflecting some stray candle flame. "You actually thought I would have fathered a child and refused to acknowledge it? You actually believed I would have married you, right under the nose of my lover, the mother of my child?"

His hands tightened on her like steel bands. "Good God, Darcy—what kind of man do you think I am?"

"I didn't know what to think," she said. When he denied her worst fear, with such conviction in his voice, such anger in his eyes, she wondered if she might have been wrong.

"You seemed so close to them. I saw you on the beach once or twice. And when I saw her at our wedding, she looked so... angry." She remembered Connie's pretty face, contorted with unhappiness.

"She was," he said, nodding grimly. "She was angry right from the beginning, when I told her you'd be staying at Two Palms, and she was furious when we got married."

Darcy swallowed and tried to be fair. "I think I can understand. She loves you..."

He shook his head grimly. "No, she doesn't. She hasn't loved me for years. I'm not sure she ever did. But she's never been a very strong person, and the past few years have been tough for her."

"And so, of course, she turned to you." Darcy tried not to sound sarcastic, but her pain was too great to hide completely.

"Yes, she did. I was the only one she had. We've been friends since we were children. She knew the romance was over, really over, between us, but she still needed my friendship."

He must have seen the disbelief in her eyes, for his voice grew more insistent. "It's true, Darcy. We aren't lovers. She was just frightened, I suppose, afraid of losing her crutch, afraid that you might not want to share me with her."

"I didn't," she whispered. "I hated to think of you with her."

"I wasn't with her. Not like that." He looked bitter, lines furrowed deep on either side of his wide mouth. "Why didn't you just ask me? I would never have guessed you gave a damn. You always seemed so indifferent."

"I didn't think I had the right. You seemed so close—there was such a family feeling between you. And you and I..." Tears were so close to the surface she almost couldn't speak. "You and I were just an arrangement. A business deal."

A muscle twitched at the edge of his jaw. "Is that all it was to you? A bargain?"

"How could I let it be more?" she cried. "Trevor was always there. And he reminded me of...of someone. Something. It hurt, because I knew it must be you."

Cursing, he released her suddenly and flung himself away, as though he didn't trust himself near her.

"No, damn it. It wasn't me."

He stood by the blockaded sliding glass doors, his arms on his hips. "It was George." The words dropped like a small, deadly bomb into the center of the room. "That's who Trevor reminds you of. He reminds you of George."

"George?" Her head swam, and she had to sit down. Even the wall couldn't hold her up now. But the darkness was taking over as the candles died, one by one, and so she groped for a chair, hands out before her like a blind person. "George?"

"Yes." He prowled the shuttered room, his harsh breathing loud, echoing in the emptiness. "George. He's partly why Connie and I never married—not that we were really right for each other, anyway. We'd been engaged for a couple of months, and then, when things were rocky between us, she met George—handsome, blue-eyed, black-hearted George. He swept her off her feet. They were together for about two years. And then Connie got pregnant.''

As though the claustrophobia had finally over-whelmed him, he snapped the lock on the sliding glass door and swung it open. But tall pieces of plywood had been nailed over the outside, and only a trickle of fresh air seeped in.

He faced the wood, as though he could see through it to the beach beyond. ''George offered her money for an abortion. By that time he had his sights set on mar-rying your mother, you see, and he didn't intend to have his plans spoiled by a little island girl and her brat.''

Suddenly, with strong, angry hands, he knocked a corner of the plywood loose, and the cool, rain-damp breeze poured in. Darcy was grateful for the reviving air. She noticed with dull surprise that there was no sound of rain. No real wind, either—only the lethargic rustle of palm fronds in a dying breeze. The hurricane had passed them by.

''So that's why you hate George,'' she said numbly. She didn't for a minute doubt the truth of the story. As if offering itself as proof, the image of Trevor's blue eyes floated before her mind's eye. That was what had haunted her, those cocky, smiling blue eyes. But they looked so different in the child, so innocent and hon-est. No wonder she hadn't realized what she was seeing.

''And that's why you wanted to marry me, isn't it? It wasn't your company's stock, at all. It was revenge, pure and simple. He took the girl you loved, so you took his stepdaughter. I was just the pawn, after all.''

He struck at the plywood again, his anger giving him amazing strength. With a thundering slam, the wood fell free, revealing the soggy, moonlit scene beyond. The patio deck glistened and smelled of sodden wood. The bushes drooped, exhausted by the beating they had taken. The beach was littered with the detritus of the storm—branches, leaves, shells, seaweed, a thousand things lost and broken.

Miles was only a silhouette against that battered backdrop, but his frustration was a living force in the room.

"No, dammit! She isn't 'the girl I love.' Haven't you been listening to a word I've said?" His voice was harsh, propelling itself into the room, assailing her where she sat.

"I married you because I thought you were the most beautiful thing I had ever seen," he went on. "I married you because, having touched you, I knew I'd never want to touch another woman."

He finally turned away from the window and faced her. His face was so harsh it was hard to believe he had just said such things.

"God knows I didn't want to feel that way about you. I told myself I knew your type all too well. You were just another sweet-faced liar, like my mother, like Connie, like a hundred women I've known and despised. A liar, a user, a cheat. I told you I preferred my women to be openly selfish, and I meant it. That way I knew what I was dealing with and no one would get hurt."

"But with women like that it's hopeless, Miles," she said, working hard to speak around the lump in her throat. "There's no chance for love."

He nodded grimly. "Exactly. Love wasn't for me, I told myself. Love was for innocents like Emily and Evan—or like Tessa."

She blinked against hot tears. "I know," she said weakly. "I think I must have felt that way, too. I never expected to fall in love."

"That's why you were willing to marry Evan."

"Yes." She bowed her head. "I had given up hope of anything more, until . . ."

"Until what?"

She moved restlessly away from him. "Until you . . . until we—"

"Until *us?* Is that what you're saying, Darcy?" He squinted at her, as if trying to hide the expression in his eyes. "Are you saying you fell in love with *me?*"

She faced him squarely, prepared for his contempt. "Yes," she said defiantly. "Ironic, isn't it? I couldn't force myself to fall in love with a man who adored me, and I can't keep myself from loving the man who despises me."

"Despises you?" In an instant, he was behind her, his hands sliding up under her arms and over her shoulders, pulling her against him. His heart beat hard and deep against her back.

"Oh, Darcy, darling—my God! Did you really not know that I love you? Not even after last night?"

She turned in his arms, facing him with eyes wide. A strange, fluttering flush, like the beating of small hot wings, was covering her body, her face. "Love me?" she repeated stupidly. "You really love me?"

"Really." He smiled. "Desperately." Strong hands cupped her face. "Insanely. And, until this very moment, I thought hopelessly."

"But you never said—"

"How could I?" His hands tightened against her cheeks. "For the longest time I didn't even know it myself. I didn't want to know it. You'd come here to marry my brother. You agreed to marry me only because you were desperate and had nowhere else to turn. You clearly didn't care about me—you wouldn't let me near you."

She shook her head mutely, unable to believe, unwilling to believe, for fear it was all a dream or a lie or anything she couldn't trust.

"I was afraid to," she began.

"Because of George?"

She shook her head. "Oh, no, no. Because of how you made me feel. I was afraid it would be too hard to lose you when it was all over. Only three years—that was all I was to have of you. I knew it wouldn't be enough for me, if I let myself care about you. If I let you make love to me...."

He laughed, a low, wonderful sound, and slid his hands down her back. "Oh, you goose. Do you know what I was thinking? That my time was running out. And last night, when you were outside with Evan, I heard you say it had all been a mistake. I think I went a little crazy then. I said such horrible things, Darcy—I was mad with jealousy, and I didn't even know what was happening to me. Can you ever forgive me?"

"But—" she still frowned, afraid to believe. "Tonight, you still seemed so angry. You said Trevor wouldn't have been in danger if you hadn't married me. You sounded as though you wished you had never done it...."

"Oh, no, darling." His face clouded over, and he shook his head and swore. "Is that what you thought I meant? I must have been half mad with worry. It was my own stupidity that had infuriated me. I should have known George would do anything to keep you from getting hold of Skyler stock. Why, even Connie knew—that's why she was so afraid. He wanted to prove our marriage was a sham, so he went straight to Connie, to ask her to testify that she and I were still lovers, to get her to say my marriage to you was merely a business ploy."

"But she refused?"

"Yes," he said slowly, "she refused. I think maybe Connie was right when she said she'd grown up. There was a time when she couldn't have stood up to him. But she told George she'd never help him. That she and I hadn't been lovers for years, since before she met him."

"That must have made him very angry."

"Furious. And you know how vicious George can be when he's thwarted. He was shouting at Connie, shoving her, and Trevor saw it all."

"Oh, no." She knew all too well that Trevor's fear must have been horrible. "Poor little boy."

"Yes," he agreed soberly. "It must have been awful. He's a brave little kid, though. He ran away looking for help. I've been a sort of uncle to him ever since he was born, so he was trying to find me. But he didn't know his way here. He got lost and was scared to death."

"Oh, no!" Her heart raced. "How terrible!"

He looked down at her soberly. "That's why I felt so responsible. I should have warned Connie that George was on the island. But I was too wrapped up in my own life to think of it. I thought you and I had finally found each other, and I could only think of you."

She flushed, remembering last night, remembering his hands against her skin, the rainbow of passion.

Suddenly his fingers were beneath her chin, gently nudging her. "Look at me," he said gruffly. Her lids drifted open, and she looked straight into his deep brown eyes. "I love you," he said. "Maybe I have, right from the beginning. That first night out in the pool, I thought I was trying to teach you a lesson. But the minute I got you in my arms I wanted you—I never wanted to let go. When I thought of you and Evan, it made me crazy with jealousy. So I told myself I hated you, that you were trying to ruin Evan's life just to get your hands on that stock."

He brushed a soft kiss on her forehead. "I was horrible, wasn't I? I'm so sorry. There's no excuse—except that no woman has ever made me feel the way you do, and I was terrified."

Strangely, she knew exactly what he meant. Terrified of the implications, frightened of the vulnerability it implied—she had hidden the truth from herself, too. They had both stood there, bloodlessly listing all the sensible reasons for getting married—and all the while the same magical, irrational, helpless flood of love and desire had been coursing through them both.

His fingers traveled up to her lips and followed the curve of the tentative smile that had formed there. He smiled, too. "Does this mean you forgive me?"

Her smiled deepened as a profound sense of peace seeped through her. Of course she forgave him. Freed of her numbing fears, she could feel love in his fingertips, could hear it in his voice. The clouds that had stood between them were finally blowing away.

She let her answer show in her eyes, and when his lips fell to her cheek, happiness was a shooting star inside her.

"I hope this doesn't mean we have to give up our plan to roust George," she said as his lips moved down her throat, a devilish mischief rippling through her voice.

"Oh?" His fingers explored her ear, and shivers traced down her arm, across her chest. "What do you have in mind?"

"Oh, all the regular things—my company, your stock." She turned her head and nibbled at his finger. It was rough and warm and salty against her tongue. "Once we get all the money under our control, it shouldn't be too hard to tame George. Let's send him to some remote island somewhere—so far away he can't ever hurt Connie or Trevor or Tessa again. Maybe he can manage the first Skyler Department Store on Bali, selling coconuts and grass skirts."

He laughed, low and delighted, then pulled her close, burying his face in the hollow of her neck.

"And we'll just explain that he'll get his rather small paycheck, regular as clockwork," she said, grinning into his thick hair, "as long as he behaves himself and grants us custody of Tessa."

"You're quite a woman, Mrs. Hawthorne," he murmured against her skin. "And I love you very much."

Lifting his head, she twined her hands into his damp hair. "Show me," she whispered. "Show me again how beautiful it can be."

His arms tightened, and she felt the beat of his heart speed up, as though happiness shot like adrenaline through his body. His lips lowered, parted and met hers with all the hungry love he had promised. And as his hot lips moved on hers, the storm revisited her. She heard the wind, felt its power lifting her. Jagged streaks of lightning crossed and recrossed her mid-section, and she felt her body melting in the rain.

But that other sound...it was wrong. It was the ringing of the telephone.

He lifted his lips from hers reluctantly, and she saw the moonlight reflected in the deep brown of his beautiful eyes. "It it's Evan, I'll kill him."

She smiled and leaned her head drowsily against the chair. It didn't matter who it was. No one could come between them now.

"We could just ignore it," he said, looking daggers at the phone.

"Then they'd probably drive back to the island to check on us," she said, chuckling.

"Damn." He stood and yanked the receiver up to his ear. "Hello," he said, the way a lion might welcome a missionary.

"Oh, hello, Tessa." He raised his brows at Darcy, who just shook her head lethargically. "No, she can't come to the phone right now. Yes, she's fine. Dammit, she's fine! Or she will be if you two pests will just leave us alone!"

He grunted, frustration getting the better of what manners he had left. "It's late, Tessa. Go to bed. And don't call back. I think the phone lines are going down—right now." And, hanging up emphatically, he pulled the phone jack from the wall, its cord popping out of the module effortlessly.

Darcy smiled dreamily as he came back to her, standing behind her chair and resting his hands on her shoulders.

"Is it always this beautiful after a hurricane?" she asked, watching the moon shimmer on the tired water. Raindrops sparkled on branches and fronds, as though heaven had spilled a jar of silver glitter.

His hands massaged her neck, her arms. "Yes," he said thickly, his fingers slipping down her collarbone to slide across her breasts. "There will be a rainbow in the morning."

Reaching up, she pulled his head back down to hers. "I can't wait until the morning," she whispered. "Make me a rainbow tonight."

HARLEQUIN
American Romance®

THE ROMANCE THAT STARTED IT ALL!

For Diane Bauer and Nick Granatelli, the walk down the aisle was a rocky road....

Don't miss the romantic prequel to WITH THIS RING—

I THEE WED
BY ANNE McALLISTER

Harlequin American Romance #387

Let Anne McAllister take you to Cambridge, Massachusetts, to the night when an innocent blind date brought a reluctant Diane Bauer and Nick Granatelli together. For Diane, a smoldering attraction like theirs had only one fate, one future—marriage. The hard part, she learned, was convincing her intended....

Watch for Anne McAllister's I THEE WED, available *now* from Harlequin American Romance.

ITW

If you loved American Romance #387
I THEE WED ...

You are cordially invited to attend the
wedding of Diane Bauer and
Nick Granatelli....

With This Ring

ONE WEDDING—FOUR LOVE STORIES FROM YOUR FAVORITE HARLEQUIN AUTHORS!

BETHANY CAMPBELL
BARBARA DELINSKY
BOBBY HUTCHINSON
ANN McALLISTER

*The church is booked, the reception arranged and the
invitations mailed. All Diane and Nick have to do is walk
down the aisle. Little do they realize that the most cherished
day of their lives will spark so many romantic notions....*

Available wherever Harlequin books are sold.

HW3

HARLEQUIN
Romance

This May, travel to Egypt with Harlequin Romance's FIRST CLASS title #3126, A FIRST TIME FOR EVERYTHING by Jessica Steele.

A little excitement was what she wanted. So Josslyn's sudden assignment to Egypt came as a delightful surprise. Pity she couldn't say the same about her new boss.

Thane Addison was an overbearing, domineering slave driver. And yet sometimes Joss got a glimpse of an entirely different sort of personality beneath his arrogant exterior. It was enough that Joss knew despite having to work for this brute of a man, she wanted to stay.

Not that Thane seemed to care at all what his temporary secretary thought about him....

HARLEQUIN'S WISHBOOK
SWEEPSTAKES RULES & REGULATIONS
NO PURCHASE NECESSARY TO ENTER OR RECEIVE A PRIZE

1. To enter the Sweepstakes and join the Reader Service, affix the Four Free Books and Free Gifts sticker along with both of your Sweepstakes stickers to the Sweepstakes Entry Form. If you do not wish to take advantage of our Reader Service, but wish to enter the Sweepstakes only, do not affix the Four Free Books and Free Gifts sticker; affix only the Sweepstakes stickers to the Sweepstakes Entry Form. Incomplete and/or inaccurate entries are ineligible for that section or sections of prizes. Torstar Corp. and its affiliates are not responsible for mutilated or unreadable entries or inadvertent printing errors. Mechanically reproduced entries are null and void.

2. Whether you take advantage of this offer or not, on or about April 30, 1992 at the offices of Marden-Kane Inc., Lake Success, NY, your Sweepstakes number will be compared against a list of winning numbers generated at random by the computer. However, prizes will only be awarded to individuals who have entered the Sweepstakes. In the event that all prizes are not claimed, a random drawing will be held from all qualified entries received from March 30, 1990 to March 31, 1992, to award all unclaimed prizes. All cash prizes (Grand to Sixth), will be mailed to the winners and are payable by check in U.S. funds. Seventh prize to be shipped to winners via third-class mail. These prizes are in addition to any free, surprise or mystery gifts that might be offered. Versions of this sweepstakes with different prizes of approximate equal value may appear in other mailings or at retail outlets by Torstar Corp. and its affiliates.

3. The following prizes are awarded in this sweepstakes: ★ Grand Prize (1) $1,000,000; First Prize (1) $25,000; Second Prize (1) $10,000; Third Prize (5) $5,000; Fourth Prize (10) $1,000; Fifth Prize (100) $250; Sixth Prize (2,500) $10; ★ ★ Seventh Prize (6,000) $12.95 ARV.

   ★ This Sweepstakes contains a Grand Prize offering of a $1,000,000 annuity. Winner will receive $33,333.33 a year for 30 years without interest totalling $1,000,000.

   ★ ★ Seventh Prize: A fully illustrated hardcover book published by Torstar Corp. Approximate Retail Value of the book is $12.95.

   Entrants may cancel the Reader Service at anytime without cost or obligation to buy (see details in center insert card).

4. Extra Bonus! This presentation offers two extra bonus prizes valued at a total of $33,000 to be awarded in a random drawing from all qualified entries received by March 31, 1992. No purchase necessary to enter or receive a prize. To qualify, see instructions on the insert card. Winner will have the choice of merchandise offered or a $33,000 check payable in U.S. funds. All other published rules and regulations apply.

5. This Sweepstakes is being conducted under the supervision of Marden-Kane, Inc., an independent judging organization. By entering this Sweepstakes, each entrant accepts and agrees to be bound by these rules and the decisions of the judges, which shall be final and binding. Odds of winning in the random drawing are dependent upon the total number of entries received. Taxes, if any, are the sole responsibility of the winners. Prizes are nontransferable. All entries must be received at the address printed on the reply card and must be postmarked no later than 12:00 MIDNIGHT on March 31, 1992. The drawing for all unclaimed Sweepstakes prizes and for the Bonus Sweepstakes Prize will take place May 30, 1992, at 12:00 NOON at the offices of Marden-Kane, Inc., Lake Success, NY.

6. This offer is open to residents of the U.S., the United Kingdom, France and Canada, 18 years or older, except employees and their immediate family members of Torstar Corp., its affiliates, subsidiaries, and all other agencies and persons connected with the use, marketing or conduct of this Sweepstakes. All Federal, State, Provincial and local laws apply. Void wherever prohibited or restricted by law. Any litigation within the Province of Quebec respecting the conduct and awarding of a prize in this publicity contest must be submitted to the Régie des Loteries et Courses du Québec.

7. Winners will be notified by mail and may be required to execute an affidavit of eligibility and release, which must be returned within 14 days after notification or an alternative winner will be selected. Canadian winners will be required to correctly answer an arithmetical skill-testing question administered by mail, which must be returned within a limited time. Winners consent to the use of their names, photographs and/or likenesses for advertising and publicity in conjunction with this and similar promotions without additional compensation.

8. For a list of our major winners, send a stamped, self-addressed envelope to: WINNERS LIST, c/o MARDEN-KANE, INC., P.O. BOX 701, SAYREVILLE, NJ 08871. Winners Lists will be fulfilled after the May 30, 1992 drawing date.

ALTERNATE MEANS OF ENTRY: Print your name and address on a 3″ ×5″ piece of plain paper and send to:

In the U.S.
Harlequin's WISHBOOK Sweepstakes
3010 Walden Ave.
P.O. Box 1867, Buffalo, NY 14269-1867

In Canada
Harlequin's WISHBOOK Sweepstakes
P.O. Box 609
Fort Erie, Ontario L2A 5X3

LTY-H491RRD

HARLEQUIN
American Romance®

RELIVE THE MEMORIES....

All the way from turn-of-the-century Ellis Island to the future of the
'90s...**A CENTURY OF AMERICAN ROMANCE** takes you on a
nostalgic journey through the twentieth century.

Watch for all the **A CENTURY OF AMERICAN ROMANCE** titles coming to you one per month over the next two months in Harlequin American Romance, including #385 MY ONLY ONE by Eileen Nauman, in April.

Don't miss a day of **A CENTURY OF AMERICAN ROMANCE**.

The women...the men...the passions...the memories....

If you missed #345 AMERICAN PIE, #349 SATURDAY'S CHILD, #353 THE GOLDEN RAIN-
TREE, #357 THE SENSATION, #361 ANGELS WINGS, #365 SENTIMENTAL JOURNEY, #369
STRANGER IN PARADISE, #373 HEARTS AT RISK, or #377 TILL THE END OF TIME and would
like to order them, send your name, address, and zip or postal code, along with a check or
money order for $2.95 plus 75¢ postage and handling ($1.00 in Canada) *for each book or-
dered,* payable to Harlequin Reader Service, to:

In the U.S.
3010 Walden Ave.
Box 1325
Buffalo, NY 14269-1325

In Canada
P.O. Box 609
Fort Erie, Ontario
L2A 5X3

Please specify book title(s) with your order.
Canadian residents please add applicable federal and provincial taxes.

CA-80

Harlequin Intrigue®

A SPAULDING & DARIEN MYSTERY
by Robin Francis

An engaging pair of amateur sleuths—Jenny Spaulding and Peter Darien—were introduced to Harlequin Intrigue readers in #147, BUTTON, BUTTON (Oct. 1990). Jenny and Peter will return for further spine-chilling romantic adventures in April 1991 in #159, DOUBLE DARE in which they solve their next puzzling mystery. Two other books featuring Jenny and Peter will follow in the A SPAULDING AND DARIEN MYSTERY series.

IBB-1A